MISADVENTURES

WITH A

COUNTRY BOY

BY
ELIZABETH HAYLEY

Mar 19

MISADVENTURES

WITH A
COUNTRY BOY

BY
ELIZABETH HAYLEY

WATERHOUSE PRESS

To all of the people who've fallen in love with an on-the-run drifter, hopefully your story worked out as well as Cole and Brooke's will. Enjoy.

CHAPTER ONE

Cole squeezed the handle of the gas pump and leaned heavily against the bed of his red Chevy pickup as he took in the scenery—long stretches of farmland and an obvious lack of civilization. It didn't matter that he was a thousand miles from home. Somehow the Kansas landscape too closely resembled the small Georgia town where he'd grown up.

He sure as hell hadn't driven eighteen hours straight for a reminder of the place he'd left. Shaking his head slowly, he didn't know what he'd find in Oregon or any place after it, but he knew it wouldn't be any place like this. He grabbed the brim of his cap and pulled it farther down to block the sun, and then he closed his eyes. A few more hours and he'd give himself the break he desperately needed and allow himself a night of rest.

He thought back to two years ago when he'd been overseas, wondering how he'd been able to do some of the things that had seemed so easy to him then. Staying awake for days at a time, walking miles with fifty pounds of gear on his back. Maybe it was the adrenaline, or maybe it was the fact that it was his job that had made it all feel so natural.

But now, as he pinched the bridge of his nose and clenched his eyes shut even harder, all of that seemed foreign, like he'd been remembering a movie he'd seen instead of a past he'd *lived*.

When he felt the gas pump shut off, Cole returned the nozzle to its holder and fastened the gas cap. Then he headed into the convenience store. Coffee from a local gas station wasn't his first choice, but it would suffice. If he could drink the tar they served in the army, he could certainly tolerate whatever this place offered.

The bell on the glass door jingled at his entrance, but the clerk didn't look in his direction as Cole headed toward the other side of the store. The middle-aged man seemed busy with another customer at the counter.

Cole poured himself a cup of black coffee and took a sip, wincing when the scalding liquid hit his tongue. He hadn't expected it to be any hotter than lukewarm. He put the lid on and grabbed a flimsy cardboard sleeve to put around the cup before heading up a nearby aisle. He took his time, enjoying the air conditioning he'd miss as soon as he got back on the road. He grabbed a bag of chips, a protein bar, and an apple on his way to the register. Cole took his place behind the woman who had been there when he'd walked in.

"Isn't there any other way to do this?" she asked. She whipped her head toward the door as she gestured toward the parking lot, frustration evident in her tone. "You should be happy to sell it."

The man sitting behind the counter crossed his arms above his round belly, which was covered by a faded white T-shirt, and stared blankly at her. "I'm sorry. I already told you. I can't sell you a car unless you have ID."

"But I've got money." The woman reached into the backpack she had slung on her shoulder and took out a wad of cash. She tossed the money onto the counter. "That's a thousand bucks," she said. "Just take it. Please."

Cole wondered if she had more than that. She couldn't possibly be offering the guy everything she had. If she was, she wasn't too bright. Money would get her a helluva lot farther than that rusty Honda would.

Cole reached into his back pocket to remove his wallet, getting ready to toss some cash on the counter and head outside, but just as he pulled the money out, the man spoke again.

"Listen, honey, you seem a little new to how the world works. Laws are put in place for a reason. It's simple. No ID, no car. I can't transfer the title without it." Now the man's palms were on the counter as he used it to push himself up so he towered over her.

The way the man used his size to intimidate a female flipped a switch in Cole he couldn't shut off. So he slipped the five back into his wallet and waited. The last thing he wanted to do was get involved. He had his own problems to deal with. He didn't have the desire to deal with someone else's. But he also couldn't leave without making sure the woman was okay.

"Fine." She snatched the wad of cash from the counter and tossed a few dollars at the man to pay for the items she'd brought to the register. Then, after grabbing the bags, she turned abruptly and shoved open the glass door.

After she exited the store, Cole watched her turn left and disappear out of sight. He wondered how she'd even gotten to Kansas. She obviously didn't have a car. Or at least one that worked. He craned his neck toward the door, hoping to see where she'd gone, but he couldn't.

"Women." The man shook his head and rolled his eyes.

Cole paid for his items quickly and left the store. Walking casually to his truck, he glanced back over his shoulder. And that was when he saw her. She was sitting on the concrete, her head buried in her hands as her body slumped in what he identified as defeat.

Cole stopped in his tracks and turned to face her. She rested her head against the store's worn brick exterior. Her eyes were closed, and her chest rose and fell rapidly. Fingers balled into tight fists, she looked like she was trying to slow her breathing as she took in deep, shaky breaths of humid air.

His conscience urged him to ask her if she was okay, if there was anything he could do to help, but the vibe she emanated wasn't exactly friendly. Cole wasn't typically one to ignore his instincts, so he remained rooted to the spot.

He was still debating what to do when the girl opened her eyes, her dark stare pinning him in place before he even had a chance to move. "What?" Her question was simple, but her tone wasn't. It held the defensiveness he imagined a wounded animal would have were it to speak—as though she were trying to maintain her ferocity even though she was emotionally bleeding out.

"Sorry, I... Are you okay?" He took a few steps toward her and, without taking his eyes off her, pointed to his truck. "You need a ride or somethin'?"

"I need a car, not a ride."

Hoping to break the tension a bit, Cole gave her a small smile. "Is there really much of a difference?"

"Yeah. Only one of them involves a stranger." The wariness on her face seemed out of place. Her look was more high school sweetheart than woman who frequented back-road gas stations. Her tiny stature didn't help harden her, though the glare she was shooting him did. This girl clearly didn't want help from some random guy at a gas station. Cole couldn't say he blamed her.

"Hi. I'm Cole," he said, extending his hand. "You tell me your name, and then we won't be strangers anymore."

She remained silent and gave him a withering look.

"Fine." He shrugged. "If you're not gonna tell me your name, I'll pick one for you." Cole studied the girl from head to toe. She wore a gray T-shirt with a neck so wide it hung off one shoulder—the kind of T-shirt people paid a hundred dollars for. He would have gladly stretched out one of his shirts for a fraction of that price. She'd paired the overpriced shirt with tight blue jeans and black flats. The way she crossed her arms over her chest and impatiently tapped her foot reminded him of some of the girls from his hometown. Girls who wouldn't give a guy the time of day if he didn't drive a flashy car. Back home, a girl like her would have taken one look at a guy like him—his beat-up ride, the dirt under his nails—and acted like a, well... "Let's go with Princess," Cole said, a faint smile on his lips.

She narrowed her eyes at him. "Not even close."

"What is it, then?"

Her gaze darted down to a twig beside her. She picked it up and tossed it a few feet away. "Rose," she said, though she didn't move to shake his hand. She looked him up and down, her expression making it clear she was still suspicious. "You're still a stranger."

Cole retracted his hand and slid it into his back pocket. "So tell me, then. How do I *stop* being a stranger?" He wasn't at all sure why he cared. Better judgment should have had him getting into his truck and driving away from this girl's drama. But his conscience wouldn't let him.

"You don't. You think just because we know each other's names that I should suddenly trust that you won't kill me later?"

Cole let out a loud laugh. She was funny...he'd give her that. And she was still Princess as far as he was concerned because the name Rose was bullshit. The quirk of her lips and the way she averted her eyes told him she wasn't being honest. At least he didn't think so. "You think I might kill you?"

She shrugged. "I don't know that you won't. Just because you have this whole...charming Southern thing going on"—she gestured up and down Cole's body with her hand—"doesn't mean you're not the next Ted Bundy."

"You think I'm charming?"

She rolled her eyes and huffed as if the question annoyed her. But Cole knew by the faint flush on her cheeks it hadn't. "I also said I think you might be the next Ted Bundy."

"I might also be Prince Charming."

Princess's expression softened, and the corners of her lips turned up slightly.

"Is that a smile?"

"No," she replied. Though he was certain she knew just as well as he did that it was.

"Listen, I'm honestly trying to help. You seem like you're trying to get someplace, and I'm headed out west but have no specific time I need to be there by, so... But I understand if you don't want to take a ride from some dude you met at a gas station. It pretty much goes against everything you've probably been taught your whole life."

Cole hesitated for a moment when another truck pulled into the station and a rowdy group of guys poured out of it. He caught one of them eyeing up Princess as he went to talk to his buddy. There was no way in hell he could leave her there. She'd be a breaking-news segment within twenty-four hours if he did. "If it'll make you feel better, you can text a picture of my license to a friend or somethin'." Cole reached into his wallet and removed his license for her to take. "You know, in case I decide to do anything that might earn me some jail time."

She narrowed her eyes at him, as if deciding what to do next, before grabbing and studying his ID closely like she was looking for any information that would help make her decision clear.

"What are you looking for?" he asked.

"That doesn't really look like you." She unwrapped an orange Starburst from the pack she held in her hand and popped it into her mouth. She chewed slowly as she twisted the wrapper around her index finger.

"Well, it is. Same guy, different hair," Cole said, removing his hat to show her his hair. "Normally it's a little longer, like this."

She stood and leaned against the building, pressing one foot back on the dusty brick behind her. Tearing the Starburst pack open some more, she held it out to him.

"Thanks," he said, taking one.

Then she took out another orange one before shoving the pack into her bag and removing her phone. She turned it on and pressed a few buttons.

Cole gestured to the ancient flip phone she was holding. There was no way that was the one she normally carried with her. "Did you teleport here from 2002 or something?"

She stopped fidgeting with the buttons and glanced up at him, her long black lashes framing her deep brown eyes perfectly. "Or something," she replied. Then she directed her attention back to the phone while Cole waited.

When she was done, she handed his license back to him and slid her phone back into the outside pocket of her backpack. She slung it over her shoulder and eyed him warily. "Okay, Cole Timmons from 116 North Washington Street, Samson, Georgia. I know where you live. And now so does my sister. So don't do anything crazy."

Cole raised his hands out to his sides innocently. "Wouldn't dream of it. Besides," he added, "I'm not the one with no ID who's carrying around a burner phone and eating only the *orange* Starbursts. If one of us is crazy, it's sure as hell not me."

She was silent for a moment before pushing off the wall and heading toward Cole's truck. And this time she didn't try to hide her smile.

Cole walked to the passenger side and stood in front of it, blocking his new companion from opening the door.

Her eyes shot to his. "What?"

He set his hands on his hips and looked at her with the hard stare he'd learned first from his father and then from the military. "I have one condition for you ridin' with me."

She returned his glare, pulling her shoulders back and raising her eyebrows.

"I'm gonna need to know your real name."

He noticed her body stiffen slightly, her stare piercing his as if she were deciding whether to ask him how he'd known she'd been lying. But she didn't. At least for now. Instead, she released a long sigh, and some of the tension seemed to slip from her body as she extended a hand. "Brooke."

He grasped her petite hand in his. "Pleased to meet you, Brooke."

She smiled but quickly shook her head as if to erase the action. "Can we go now?"

"Sure thing." Cole pulled the door open for her before walking around the truck and climbing into the driver's side.

"I hope your Southern twang doesn't mean you're going to force me to listen to country music for the entire drive," Brooke said.

And as he fired up the engine and the voice of Blake Shelton blared through the speakers, he couldn't help but laugh at the look of pain that flashed across Brooke's face. He may enjoy having a passenger after all.

◆ ◆ ◆ ◆

Brooke sat in the passenger seat, forcing her muscles to relax and her breathing to stay even. Truth was, she was a fucking wreck. But damned if she'd let the Boy Scout next to her know

15

that. Brooke could do cool, calm, and collected. It was an act she'd perfected after years of having to appear unaffected in a world of cold, manipulative people.

Getting in the car with Cole had been a reckless decision born out of a need to stay on the move. Without any better options, she'd had to take the chance and trust a cute guy with a kind smile. At least looking at him wouldn't be a hardship. The fact he hadn't recognized her was a big selling point as well. Through his faded red T-shirt and worn jeans, Brooke could make out a solid build that more likely came from hard work than a gym membership. She just hoped he was as nice as he seemed. Despite how many times in her life she'd made the threat in jest, she didn't *actually* want to die.

She watched the landscape whip by as they drove. Suddenly, she realized there was an important question she'd neglected to ask. "Where are we going?"

Cole scratched the side of his neck. "Well, *I'm* heading to Oregon. I guess you're going wherever you tell me to drop you between here and there." He flashed her a smile that revealed almost perfect teeth—save for a slightly crooked canine—and dimples.

Of course he has dimples. Brooke surveyed the man as he drove, trying to get a better read on him. She remembered his handshake: solid and strong. Dependable. And his smile was broad and open. He was the kind of guy who made a person want to lean on him. To turn themselves over to him for safekeeping.

But Brooke wasn't one to fall for that. She'd learned at an early age that the firmer the handshake, the less genuine the intentions. The wider the smile, the more deceitful the lies. She hadn't only been warned of this truth—she'd seen it, lived it.

She glanced at Cole again. Despite her reticence, she didn't *feel* like he was dangerous. And since she had little else to go on, she'd have to settle for trusting her instincts. Otherwise she'd be stuck in Kansas for the foreseeable future. "What's in Oregon?"

"A friend."

Rolling her eyes at his failure to elaborate, she decided to sink back in her seat. Not talking was actually the better option anyway.

"So where am I dropping you?" Cole asked after they'd traveled in silence for a while.

Brooke thought for a moment. "I'll let you know when we get there."

Cole darted his attention to her for a moment before looking back at the road. "But how can I get there if I don't know where 'there' is?"

"There can be anywhere. Or the middle of nowhere."

Cole's face pinched together as if he were thinking. "What does that mean? It sounds like some kind of weird *Alice in Wonderland* riddle. Maybe I should've called you Alice."

Brooke scoffed. "Do I look like I fell down a rabbit hole?" From the corner of her eye, she saw Cole's mouth open to reply. She held up a hand. "Don't answer that. And you shouldn't call me that, or Princess for that matter, if you expect me to answer."

Silence descended again, but it was short-lived. "So where

did you live before you chased the white rabbit?" Cole asked.

"You're really beating this metaphor to death."

Cole shrugged. "I think it's still got some fight left in it. So?"

Brooke looked over at him. "So what?"

Cole huffed out a laugh. "Where are you from?"

"What's the difference?"

"No difference, I guess. But since we're riding together to only-you-know-where, I figured we could get to know each other a little."

Brooke inhaled sharply, hoping the air would fortify her backbone, before turning in her seat to face him. "Listen, no offense. You seem like a nice enough guy, but I'm really not interested in playing Twenty Questions. I know I made a big deal at the gas station about you being a stranger, but beyond knowing you're not going to wear my skin as a coat, I think we're good." Brooke felt bad for being so harsh to a man who'd been nothing but kind to her, but getting chummy with him couldn't happen. She was trying to disappear, not make friends.

Drumming his fingers on the steering wheel, Cole tilted his head from side to side a few times as if he were trying to puzzle something out.

Brooke sighed again. "What?"

"Nothin'. I'm just trying to figure out if I'd look silly since your skin would be small on me."

"Jesus Christ," she muttered as she stifled a laugh. No way was she letting Cole know she thought he was funny. The last thing she wanted to do was encourage conversation. She sank down in her seat a bit. "I didn't know I bummed a ride from a comedian."

Cole smiled that full, megawatt smile again. "Now there's an idea. Do you think I could make some cash at a few comedy clubs along the way? I've been told my Southern accent makes me funnier."

"It doesn't, and I wouldn't bank on it."

"Was that a pun?"

She squinted her eyes. "Was what a pun?"

"You know. I said I needed to earn money, and you said the bank thing. I thought it was clever until you made it clear it was an accident."

Brooke opened and closed her mouth a few times, unable to think of a response. This country boy was really something else. When it felt like too much time had passed for her to reply, she did the only thing she could think to do—she ignored his comment completely and took out her phone.

She waited silently as it powered on again, and once she could see she had a voicemail from her sister, she put the phone up to her ear to listen. Since she'd left Philadelphia, she'd only texted Natasha once to send her the picture of Cole's ID.

I'm safe. If anything happens to me, I'm with this guy.

Leaning against the door and away from Cole, she turned the volume down on the phone so Cole wouldn't hear her sister's message.

"Brooke, where are you?"

She could already tell Natasha's voice was hushed and worried, and that worry seemed to transfer immediately to Brooke as well. If her sister was nervous, then Brooke should have been too.

"Please tell me you're not in Kansas. Your agent said there's been a sighting of you there and that he was sending someone to check it out."

Brooke's heart sped up even more rapidly.

Shit. Swallowing the lump in her throat, she listened to the remainder of her sister's message, which told her to call as soon as she could.

Brooke shot back a quick text saying she'd call as soon as she was able and then abruptly shut off the phone. She shoved it back into her bag and zipped the pocket hastily, as if the distance between her and the call would somehow make her feel better. It didn't.

"Everything okay?" She could hear the concern in Cole's voice, but she ignored it and kept her eyes fixed on the road ahead of her. At least they were moving. For now anyway.

"Yeah. It's fine," Brooke replied, trying like hell to sound calm. She was certain she didn't. She willed herself to elaborate—to come up with some sort of a believable excuse. But as the seconds passed in silence because, once again, she had yet to come up with anything, she accepted that her terse response would have to suffice.

She stole a glance at Cole, who had one eyebrow cocked but, thankfully, didn't press her. He just reached for the radio and cranked up the volume.

Brooke wanted to feel relieved. A silent Cole was a better alternative to an inquisitive one. But the air in the truck felt tense, and by the way Cole's fingers were drumming on the steering wheel, she was sure he felt it too. Except for the radio, they drove in silence for the next fifteen minutes or so, during which Brooke obsessed about her conversation with her sister. One thing was sure: she had to get the hell out of this state as quickly as possible. And despite how anxious it made her, Brooke had no choice but to rely on Cole to make that happen. "If I promise not to be a total jerk, will you promise not to dump me anywhere?"

Cole's head swung to her quickly before he looked back at the road. "I'd never just dump you somewhere. You have my word on that." His tone sounded sincere, so she let herself believe him. For now at least.

"Thanks," she said softly.

"No problem."

"I really do appreciate it. Who knows how long I would've been stuck at the gas station before another bus rolled through."

Cole nodded but didn't say anything.

Brooke forged on. "So I have a proposition for you."

"Oh yeah?"

"Obviously I need a car, but without ID, I'm never going to be able to get one. So if you let me tag along with you, I'll fund the trip until we get to...wherever we're going." She phrased it casually, but it was a point she would be firm about. She'd been beholden to people all her life. She refused to be completely reliant on someone when this entire trip was supposed to be her chance to finally experience what it felt like to be independent.

"And what makes you think I'd take your money?" Cole asked.

Brooke's reply came out of her mouth without any consultation with her brain. "Well, your truck is kind of beat-up." A quick glance at Cole showed his knuckles whitening on the steering wheel. *So much for proving I'm not a total jerk.*

Cole didn't respond, his focus never drifting from the windshield.

Brooke wrung her hands in her lap. "Shit, I'm sorry. I didn't mean that how it sounded. Well, I mean, I guess I meant it, but I didn't mean to make it sound like a bad thing. Though, I don't know that it can be a good thing either. At least you *have* a car. I just..." Brooke stopped talking for a second and took a deep breath. "I wasn't being cryptic earlier. I don't have a destination in mind. I'm hoping I'll know it when I see it. But I figured...until I found it...that it'd be best to travel with you. Taking a bus across the rest of the country isn't really my idea of a good time. Halfway was bad enough. But I don't want to feel like I'm using you or dependent on you. I want to hold up my end of things, and money is all I have to offer."

Cole didn't move, nor did he speak for a minute. "There are other ways to get around. Like trains."

Brooke sighed and looked out her window. "True. There are trains."

Cole took a deep breath and let it out slowly. "Though I guess there's no reason you should take a train if I'm headin' in the same direction."

Brooke looked over at him, hopeful. Being on the run with Cole, even if he wasn't aware they were running, certainly felt safer than being on the run by herself.

"We can stick together. But I want to get something straight. You are never to insult Mary Sue again."

Brooke looked at him in confusion. "Who's Mary Sue?"

Cole ran a hand over the dash. "You're ridin' in her." His

lips curved at the corners after he spoke.

She was surprised by how happy she was to see him smile. So much so that she had to try to conceal her own grin from appearing. "You named your truck Mary Sue? Seriously? Could you be any more of a Southern stereotype?"

"That's not what I want to hear," he taunted.

Brooke sighed. "Okay, fine. No insulting Mary Sue."

Cole's laugh was deep with a hint of a rasp behind it. It was a genuine sound that made him, and the world, seem a little less frightening.

CHAPTER TWO

"We're staying *here*?" Brooke glanced tentatively around the motel parking lot. From what she could tell from the outside, the place didn't get much business. There were only three cars in the lot, and since one was parked directly in front of the office, she assumed it belonged to an employee.

"Yeah. Why?" Cole seemed genuinely confused about why Brooke had questioned his choice of accommodations.

Brooke nearly blurted out that she wasn't in the mood to have her stuff infested with bed bugs, but she caught herself. She needed to stop with the high-maintenance shit before she truly earned her nickname. "Uh, nothing. It's fine. Just... rustic."

Cole pulled into the spot closest to the office and turned the ignition off. He gave her that same half grin she'd seen so many times on the drive so far—the left side of his lips turning upward just enough to hint at his amusement. "Rustic, huh? For a country boy like me, rustic is a compliment."

"I didn't mean it to sound like it wasn't." She knew she sounded defensive, but dammit, she was trying so hard to not act like the spoiled brat the media always portrayed her as.

"Okay, okay, don't get your knickers in a twist," he said.

"Did you just say 'knickers'?"

Cole smiled that goofy grin that was starting to make her insides feel warm whenever he directed it at her. "My mama always used to say it. Guess it stuck with me."

Brooke found herself wanting to know more. Wanting to know about his mother who "used" to say things and who raised a man who looked like a god and sounded like a cowboy. But she didn't ask, because she didn't want to have to answer any personal questions of her own. So instead she climbed out of his truck and walked around to his side, where he joined her.

He pulled his Braves cap off his head just long enough to run a hand through his curls, which had dampened to a darker brown with sweat. He held the door open so Brooke could enter the small, dimly lit office, and when she stepped inside, she froze. There was something unnerving about being at a place like this around midnight, but Cole's presence made her feel a little more at ease. He approached the tall counter and leaned against it so he was facing Brooke as he spoke to the man working. "We need a room for the night," Cole said.

"Actually *two* rooms," Brooke spoke up.

"We don't need two rooms. That's double the price. We can just get two beds."

"I don't care about the money."

"Well, you should."

"Cole—"

"Princess." Cole tilted his head and crossed his arms, his long body relaxed against the counter.

Brooke let out an annoyed huff. "Stop calling me that. I told you my real name."

"Princess is more fitting. Plus, how do I know Brooke's

25

even your real name?"

"The same way you knew Rose *wasn't*." She kept her gaze fixed on his, hoping he would let her answer suffice.

He kept giving her that look, so she dropped his stare. She dug around for a few moments until she found what she'd been looking for. "Here," she said, thrusting her license up at him.

Cole looked confused. "So, Brooke Alba, you *do* have ID," he said, taking it from her fingers and studying it closely. "Twenty-four. Good to know."

Brooke's instinct was to tell him not to say her name out loud. It was bad enough *Cole* knew her real name. She didn't want anyone else hearing who could later verify she'd been at the motel, even if the chances of that happening were slim. She decided it wouldn't do any good to correct him now. She hadn't wanted to show her ID to the guy in the gas station, but now the damage, if there was any, had been done. "Happy?" she asked with an exaggerated eye roll.

Cole's amused smile broadened. "Very." Then he turned back to the man behind the counter. "But we still don't need two rooms."

"Cole, we just spent hours cooped up in a truck together. Maybe I want some space."

He sighed heavily but turned to the man behind the counter. "Do you have two rooms available?"

The man handed them their keys and directed them to their rooms. Brooke resisted the urge to sprint to hers. The accommodations were exactly what she had pictured when they'd pulled into the parking lot: a flimsy-looking bed in the middle of the room and a few laminate wood end tables and a desk adorning the perimeter. She could see where the veneer had started to warp in spots from people's sweating beer bottles or car keys tossed roughly onto the furniture.

She put her bag on the maroon, upholstered desk chair and plopped herself onto the bed. Trying not to think about what organisms could be lurking in a place like this, she was suddenly thankful she didn't have a black light. She made a mental note to herself to purchase a set of sheets the first chance she got. Clearly, traveling around with Cole would be without the conveniences—and cleanliness—she was used to. That thought made her feel spoiled, but she was too tired to mentally berate herself for it right then. Besides, any luxuries she was used to were ones she'd earned herself.

She'd also need to purchase some clothes. When she'd left Philadelphia, her focus had been on just that: leaving. She hadn't packed much, figuring that with the ten grand she'd taken from the bank, she'd be more than able to buy what she needed. But since she hadn't been able to get a car and she hadn't asked Cole to stop someplace, she suddenly found herself with nothing but a toothbrush and the clothes she'd been wearing for the past two days.

Somehow she found enough energy to pull herself up to her feet so she could riffle through her backpack. When she found what she was looking for, she sat back down on the edge of the bed. Her fingers traveled over the buttons of her phone as she waited for it to turn on.

When the small screen finally lit up, she hesitated, second-guessing her urge to call Natasha. But after hearing her voicemail earlier, she had to get more information. Tentatively,

Brooke dialed her sister's number and waited for her to pick up. She was getting ready to hang up when she heard Natasha's hushed voice answer.

"Brooke?"

"Shh. Don't say my name. Where are you?"

"It's fine. I'm outside. Where are *you*?"

"Middle of nowhere, USA."

"Like *Deliverance* middle of nowhere or *Texas Chainsaw Massacre* middle of nowhere?" her sister asked.

"That's a helpful comparison. I can't wait to go to sleep now." Brooke rubbed her eyes with her fingers. "Did they get any new information?"

"No. I heard Dad cursing earlier. You were seen on a bus but got off in Kansas, and no one has seen you since."

Brooke heaved a sigh of relief. "Thank God."

"It's getting kind of intense...seeing the lengths they're going to to find you." Her sister took in a deep breath. "Is all this... Are you sure it's worth it? It was all well and good to talk about, but now that it's happening, it feels really dangerous. I mean, you're driving around with a total stranger. What if he tries to sell you into an underground trafficking ring?"

Clearly, her morbid sense of humor was hereditary. "It's fine. *I'm* fine. I just... I had to get away. Coming back isn't an option right now."

The line was quiet for a moment before Natasha spoke. "You're okay, though, right?"

"Yeah, I'm fine. We stopped at a motel for the night. I'm gonna try to get some rest. I just wanted to let you know I'm okay." Brooke paused for a moment and dropped her head.

"Better than I'd be if I were home."

"Yeah, I know." Natasha's voice was quiet, soft. Brooke knew her sister probably wanted to ask more, but she knew better. "Call when you can, okay?"

"I will. Love you."

"Love you too," Natasha answered.

Brooke waited until she heard her sister hang up before she pushed End and put the phone back in her bag. Despite its brevity, Brooke's conversation with her sister had managed to stress her out even more. As she and Cole had traveled, the distance and his easy-going personality had given her a slight sense of security. But that was a dangerous feeling to have. The reality was, she could be recognized at any time. Enough people knew who she was, it would be stupid to let her guard down.

Now she felt vulnerable, alone when she didn't need to be. She glanced over to the wall that separated her from her traveling companion since the guy at the front desk had given them adjacent rooms, and she wondered what was happening on the other side. She briefly contemplated going over, but she didn't want to wake him if he was asleep.

Thoughts of a sleepy-eyed Cole invaded her mind—his dark-blond hair rumpled even more than it was from the cap he wore, a hint of a dimple as he dreamed. Though she felt guilty about possibly waking him, the thought of staying in her room by herself any longer was worse than admitting to herself that Cole made her feel...protected? Safe? Comfortable? And right now she needed to feel those things. Even though she knew it was too soon to trust Cole completely, there was something about him that couldn't be explained through logic.

She slung her bag over her shoulder, grabbed her room key, and pulled the door closed behind her before making the short walk next door. The summer air had gotten considerably cooler since the afternoon, so she crossed her arms and extended a hand just enough to knock lightly. She'd told herself if Cole didn't answer, he was probably asleep, and she'd go back to her room. But now, as she stared at the navy-blue door and felt her stomach tighten nervously, she reconsidered her pact with herself.

Thankfully, she didn't have to reevaluate her decision because the door opened. And standing at the doorway was a shirtless Cole, his wet hair dripping as he tucked the longer pieces behind his ears. Though her eyes briefly dropped shamelessly to where Cole's hands moved to secure the corner of a towel around his chiseled hips, she willed them to refocus on him. "Hi" was all she could get out.

♦ ♦ ♦ ♦

Cole narrowed his eyes at Brooke in confusion. He hadn't expected to see her until the morning. Although he certainly wasn't complaining. If there was one thing Brooke was, it was easy on the eyes. With her long dark hair, which he would bet was as soft as it looked, and her smooth, sun-kissed skin, which made her glow, Cole could admit he was smitten. She was feisty too, which Cole definitely enjoyed. "What's goin' on?"

"Nothing. I just..." Brooke turned to the side to glance down the long balcony that ran along the outside of the rooms before quickly snapping her head back toward Cole.

"You okay?" Cole asked as he stuck his head out and peeked around the doorway. A middle-aged man a few doors down fumbled with his keys as he tried to enter his room.

"Yeah." Brooke nodded. "I'm fine. I just wanted to know if you had a shirt or something I could borrow." She pulled on the hem of the one she was wearing and looked down. "I didn't bring much with me. Or anything, really." She shook her head and laughed as she pushed her fingers through her hair and brought it around to lay on her other shoulder. "I'm sorry. I shouldn't ask, but..."

Brooke left her sentence unfinished, and it was then that Cole realized he'd been staring for what seemed like way too long without saying anything. "Don't be sorry," he blurted out. He stepped back from the door and headed over to his bag, which he'd tossed on the bed. "I have something."

It was only when he'd started to rummage through his clothes that he suddenly remembered he wasn't wearing anything but a towel. "How's this?" he asked as he held out a T-shirt and mesh shorts.

Brooke unfolded the black shirt and held it up to her frame, which looked even smaller behind the clothing. "It's perfect. Thanks," she answered with a small smile.

She turned toward the door again and moved to leave, but Cole spoke up before she got more than a few feet from him. "You want to watch TV or somethin'?" He blurted it out before he even thought about it. Logically, he knew there was something going on with Brooke that he maybe shouldn't get himself involved in. She had ID but refused to show it to buy a car. He hadn't quite figured out what to make of her attitude, her dress, her roll of cash. But he also felt oddly drawn to this complicated stranger. There was something about the way she'd hesitated when she'd turned around and the slight fall in her voice when she'd thanked him for the clothes. It made Cole recognize the loneliness in her. Loneliness that was in him too.

"Yeah, okay," Brooke answered softly. "You don't mind? You've been driving all day."

"Almost *two* days, actually." One corner of Cole's lips turned up into a partial smile. "But we don't have anyplace we got to be tomorrow, right?" He shrugged. "Stay as long as you want. We can watch whatever dumb shit they got on TV here. Checkout's not 'til noon. We can sleep late."

His smile broadened to let her know his offer was sincere, and Brooke's face seemed to brighten with it. It was one of the first times since they'd met that she actually seemed at ease.

"You mind if I take a shower first?" she asked. "I won't be long."

"Nope. Take your time." Cole watched Brooke as she turned to leave, letting his eyes wander down from her exposed shoulder to her round ass. The way it swayed back and forth just a bit as she exited his room made his cock twitch beneath his towel. *Jesus, get it together.* He couldn't perv on someone he would be stuck in a car with for who knows how long. Especially since that person was as guarded as the Federal Reserve.

The temptation was there, but he needed to keep that shit in check. And not only because it would undoubtedly make things awkward as fuck but because she was obviously running from something. An abusive boyfriend? The law? He didn't know. But whatever it was, she'd clearly left in a hurry, and he didn't want to get involved.

Cole pulled on some boxers, sweatpants, and a soft T-shirt. Before he turned on the TV, he opened his door and flipped the lock to prevent it from closing. Then he hung his towel on the bathroom door and stretched out on the bed. As much as his eyes were tempted to close, he willed them to stay open. He clicked through the channels until he found something that would hold his attention and turned up the volume. A few minutes later, he heard Brooke knock as she stepped into his room.

"You left the door open?" Brooke asked, looking at him like he was insane.

"Yeah. So you could come right in."

"But you never know..."

Cole laughed. "Oh yeah, I forgot. There are crazy people who wear their victims' organs and stuff. I'll be more careful next time," he promised.

Brooke dead-bolted the door behind her, and her face flushed a bit. "Well, it sounds ridiculous when you say it like that. I never said they'd wear the organs, just their skin."

"The skin's an organ," he replied. "The largest in our body, actually."

Brooke's eyes narrowed at him playfully as she plopped herself onto the bed next to him. "Smartass."

Cole shot her a wide grin. "Hmm...charming *and* smart. I'll take it."

"I said smart*ass*. Emphasis on the *ass* part."

"Well, I do work quite hard on it."

Brooke swatted his arm. "Stop misinterpreting me on purpose." She turned toward the TV and watched it for a moment. "What is...this?" she asked.

"What?"

"What we're watching," Brooke clarified, her eyes wide in what looked to be disgust.

"It's a show about fly fishing."

"Is this a real show? Like one that people watch?"

"Yeah," Cole answered. "*I'm* watching it, aren't I? And now so are you."

"No. I'm definitely *not* watching this." Brooke's expression turned serious as she reached for the remote.

Cole held it to the side, his long arm outstretched so it was out of Brooke's reach. "My room, my choice."

"Fishing's so boring. And watching a show about it is even worse than doing it."

Cole had to admit she had a point. "Fine. I'll change it. But we're compromisin', Princess. It has to be something we both agree on. No way I'm gettin' stuck watching some documentary on the different ways to tie a scarf."

Brooke's face remained stoic, but Cole could tell from the way the corners of her eyes crinkled a bit she was holding back a smile. "Like I don't already know how to tie a scarf," she said before lunging at him and snatching the controller from his hand.

It was the sexiest thing he'd experienced in months.

CHAPTER THREE

Cole rolled over toward the edge of the bed and stretched his long arms above him. He could tell from the thin stream of light peeking through the curtains that it was morning. Or afternoon. Since he hadn't set any sort of alarm clock, he wasn't sure how long he'd slept. Or how long *they'd* slept.

They'd watched some TV and eventually fallen asleep due to pure exhaustion. But now, with Brooke's arm lightly touching his back, Cole was suddenly wide awake.

He flipped over toward her, hoping the movement would rouse her. It didn't. Instead, she lay next to him, her chest rising and falling evenly with every breath. The hem of the oversize T-shirt he'd loaned her was pulled almost up to her ribs, allowing Cole to see her smooth skin. *Fuck.* With a view like that, he was having a difficult time getting his dick to behave.

"Do you always act this creepy in the morning?"

Cole startled at Brooke's question but then chuckled softly. "No. This is a little early for me. I usually wait 'til it starts gettin' dark."

Brooke opened her eyes and flopped onto her side to face him, propping herself on her elbow and resting her head in her hand. "What time *is* it, anyway?"

"Um, not sure." He grabbed his cell phone off the table

next to the bed and pushed the button. "Almost eleven thirty."

Brooke groaned and rubbed a hand across her face. "We have to check out in a half hour."

"I know," Cole answered, finally rising to head toward the bathroom. "Let's get dressed and get somethin' to eat after we check out."

Brooke yawned. "I want pancakes."

Cole snorted. "Of course you do, Princess." He shut the bathroom door on her reply and put his hands on the sink, leaning into them. Looking at his reflection in the mirror—taking in his morning scruff, pale-blue eyes, and disheveled blond hair—he tried to reason with himself. "She's nothin' but trouble," he murmured softly. "And trouble is the last thing you need."

Mentally, he accepted what he'd told himself. Physically, however, the image of Brooke in his bed made his cock perk up with excitement. He rubbed a calloused hand over his face before returning it to the sink, trying to get a grip on his thoughts without gripping his cock. A feat that was proving harder with every passing second.

And as if to further remind him why lusting after her was a bad idea, a loud, obnoxious knock came from the door. "I'm going back to my room. Hurry up and meet me by the truck when you're done. I'm hungry."

"You realize telling me to hurry only makes me want to go slower, right?"

She scoffed, and he could practically hear her eyes rolling. "You're such a child. And anyway, you don't have that luxury. Half an hour, remember?"

"Go away."

"Or what?" she said in a sing-songy voice that sounded more melodic than he thought possible for how annoying she was being.

Cole thought for a second. "Or I'll shave your head while you sleep."

There was a moment of silence before she spoke again. "You wouldn't do that." Her voice was the quietest he'd heard it since meeting her, as if she wasn't sure if he was serious or not.

"You don't sound so sure."

More silence. "I'll check us out and meet you at the truck."

When he heard the door close, he slid his hands off the sink countertop. After splashing some water on his face and brushing his teeth, he got dressed, grabbed his duffel, and headed down to the truck. Brooke was already there, leaning against the tailgate.

"There's a diner down the block," she said without looking at him.

"What if I don't want to go there?"

She took off her sunglasses. "Why wouldn't you?" She rested her forearm on the tailgate and shot him a withering look. "It's a diner, and everyone likes diners."

"Even royalty such as yourself?"

She stared at him for a second before lowering her gaze and shuffling her feet and then straightened her posture to look him in the eyes again. "The diner is to the right. I need to hit a mall too. This town doesn't have one, but the guy at the desk said there is one two towns over."

"I think we passed a Walmart on our way into town. Why

don't we just stop there?" Cole asked as he got in and started the engine.

The way she slowly panned toward him reminded him of *The Exorcist*. "Walmart?"

"Yeah. They have everything, and we wouldn't have to go out of our way."

"The mall isn't out of our way. I grabbed a map from the lobby. We could just go that direction to get back on the highway."

Cole knew he was being stubborn, and he really had no reason to be. He put the truck in reverse and said, "Okay, Princess. Since you're the one with the cash, the diner it is. But you're on your own at the mall. I'll wait in the truck."

He watched her inhale and fidget beside him, as though his words made her nervous, but all she said was, "Okay," before turning to stare out the window.

They drove in silence to the diner. Ate in virtual silence too. It was as if something had happened between them that had taken them a step backward, had made them more like the strangers they were.

The only talking they did on the way to the mall consisted of Brooke giving him directions she'd apparently memorized. When they arrived, he pulled into a parking space and told her he'd be there when she was done.

She opened her mouth to say something but evidently thought better of it as she threw on her sunglasses and some sort of trucker hat he didn't even know she had. Then she left the truck and walked away. Why the hell would she put on sunglasses when she hadn't had them on already and was about to enter a building? Sighing, he chalked it up to her being weird as hell and chose not to think any more about it.

When Cole saw Brooke exit the mall an hour later, he climbed out and watched her struggle with the bevy of bags she had dangling from each hand. Victoria's Secret, Nordstrom, Express, Sephora, and a bunch of other names he couldn't make out. *Jesus Christ.*

He got out and opened her door, calling upon the manners his mama had ingrained in him. She pushed her seat forward and stowed the bags behind it.

"Did you leave anything in there for the other shoppers?" he teased.

"Yup," she replied simply before tossing her hat and sunglasses on the dash. Then she pushed her seat back into place and climbed inside. She wore her irritation on her face, and he couldn't blame her. But maybe it was better that way. Despite the comfortableness they'd found the night before, they were probably better off keeping the distance Brooke had put between them when he'd picked her up. Getting close was problematic for a whole host of reasons.

Still, he couldn't keep himself from asking, "Where are you going to store it all?"

"I got a bigger duffel bag, *Dad.*"

He didn't say anything else as he closed her door and walked around to the driver's side. He pulled his phone out of his pocket to enter directions so he could continue on his journey to Oregon, only to find that it was dead. *Shit.* Cole slumped back into his seat before turning on the engine and pulling out onto the road. "Where's the map you said you got?"

"Why do you need it?"

"Why does it matter?" When she stared at him in response, he took a deep, calming breath and explained. "I must not have plugged my phone into the charger all the way. My battery's dead, so I can't look up the directions."

"You're traveling across the country, and you don't have a car charger?"

"The lighter doesn't work. I only use my phone when I need to get to a highway, and then I shut it off to save the battery." Cole looked over at her, but Brooke's eyes stayed glued to the windshield as he drove. "So can I have the map?"

Brooke looked straight ahead. "I don't have it."

"What do you mean? You said you grabbed one from the hotel lobby."

"Yeah, but I folded it up and put it in my back pocket, and it kept falling out when I tried on clothes, so I threw it away."

"Good thinking." He was pretty sure the dryness of his voice could have caused a drought, but he didn't care.

She shifted in her seat so she was facing him. "How was I supposed to know we'd need it? I'm not a psychic."

Cole sighed. "It's fine. We'll just drive. I'm sure we'll see a sign or a gas station we can pull into."

"I don't need you to tell me it's fine like you're forgiving me for something," she snapped. "I didn't do anything wrong. Besides, it's not my fault Bobbi Jo's too old to charge your phone."

Though he couldn't keep his hands from clenching the steering wheel, Cole chose not to correct her about the truck's name. He didn't need the aggravation right now. Arriving at what seemed to be a main road, he turned onto it and hoped for the best.

"Turn left at the light."

"What?" he asked.

"I may have thrown the map away, but that doesn't mean I didn't look at it. I got us to the mall without using it, didn't I? Turn left."

Cole felt in his bones he should *not* turn left. But he chalked it up to not being inclined to do anything she told him to and turned.

The farther they drove and the more turns Brooke directed him to make, the more apparent it became that Cole should've trusted his instincts. "I don't think this is right," he said as they started seeing more livestock and fewer people.

"It is. I remember."

He chanced a look over at her and observed the hard set of her jaw. He knew she would be too stubborn to admit she was wrong. And that juvenile part of himself that had emerged over the last twenty-four hours very much needed to prove just how wrong she was. So he kept driving. Pretty soon the road they were traveling on became completely deserted. "Is this still the right way?"

"Yes."

"Really, Toto? Because I'm pretty sure we're not in Kansas anymore."

Brooke slowly turned her head to face him. "I'm not a dog."

He exhaled sharply. "Can you please just admit that you don't know where the hell you're taking us?"

"I'd really rather not." There was clear defeat in her voice that would have made Cole feel bad for her if they weren't in the middle of fucking nowhere.

Cole was getting frustrated. They had gone too far and gone down too many different roads to head back the way they'd come. At least with the sun going down, he knew what direction they were heading.

They spent the next half hour driving in silence. He was thankful he'd eaten a large lunch, because it was closing in on dinnertime with no food joints in sight.

"If I were to apologize, could we forget this ever happened?" Brooke's voice was low and sincere.

But Cole was tired and hungry, two things that made him much too grumpy to let her off the hook that easily. "I'm pretty sure I'll never forget this happened."

"Never is a long time," she said as if she were truly contemplating the extent of its duration.

Cole shook his head. "I swear, I knew you were going to be trouble."

He felt her eyes on him, but he refused to turn toward her. Mostly because he knew that was a shitty thing to say, and he didn't want confirmation that he'd hurt her feelings.

"Not the first time I've been told that. Probably won't be the last either. But I truly didn't mean to be trouble for you. So if you'd just pull over, I'll get my stuff and get out of your hair." Her words were calm but held a note of steel beneath them.

"Don't be ridiculous."

"Pull over, Cole."

"I'm not going to pull over."

42

"I'm not asking. I'm telling you. Pull. The. Fuck. Over."

Cole prepared himself for oncoming drama and pulled onto the shoulder.

Brooke barely waited for him to come to a complete stop before opening her door. She quickly started pulling things out of the bags and stuffing what she could fit into her backpack and the duffel bag she'd bought.

Cole rested his wrist on the steering wheel. "What are you doing?" he asked on an exhale.

"Isn't it obvious?"

"Oh, come on. Get real." He gestured at the barren landscape before them. "Where are you gonna go?"

She zipped up her backpack and looked at him a moment before speaking. "Listen, I get that you have noble intentions, but the truth is, this was a bad idea from the start. Because I *am* trouble, and I'm better off on my own."

He snorted. "I'm sure that'll work out real well for you."

She shrugged. "Can't be any worse than what I left behind." And with that, she closed her door and began walking.

He watched her for a moment. Guilt swamped him as she stormed away. Coasting the truck alongside her, he leaned over to roll down the passenger window.

"Brooke, seriously, I can't leave you here. It's not safe."

She didn't stop or slow down. She didn't acknowledge him in any way.

"Brooke?"

Nothing.

"Get in the truck," he gritted through clenched teeth.

She continued walking, still not bothering to answer.

Cole nodded. "Okay then." He looked over his left shoulder before pulling back onto the highway and gunning the engine.

◆ ◆ ◆ ◆

Readjusting the bags on her shoulder for the fourth time in ten minutes, Brooke cursed silently. She let out a long sigh as she put her hand up above her eyes so she could see. *Yes!* It was probably still over a mile away, but she could definitely make out some sort of restaurant or store in the distance. "I may be a princess, but I can get along on my own just fine." Brooke didn't make a habit of talking to herself, but there was something about being in the middle of nowhere that made her want to hear a voice, even if it was her own.

She also knew she was saying it to try to convince herself. When she'd decided to leave home—or maybe disappear from home would have been more accurate—part of it had been to prove to herself and her family that she was capable of...something. Anything. But at the first sign of trouble, she'd done the very thing she'd promised herself she wouldn't: she let someone else be responsible for her. Cole was a good guy, which meant he definitely didn't need to be dragged into her fucked-up situation. It was bad enough she'd gotten the guy lost. That would pale in comparison to the other complications she'd bring to his life. No, she was better off on her own.

Fifteen minutes later, she walked up to a building with the word Bar written above it. The place had seen better days. The parking lot had a few cars but mostly held eighteen-wheelers. She pulled open the dark-green wooden door, its rusty hinges announcing her arrival to the men sitting at the bar. A few heads turned toward her, their beady glazed eyes narrowing in confusion at the sight of her. It was more than obvious she didn't exactly belong in a place like this. Straightening her spine, she walked toward the bar with her chin up, hoping she didn't look as intimidated as she felt.

The men seemed unimpressed and returned to their conversations, though she'd bet anything their voices were a lot quieter than they'd been before. She walked to the end of the bar where a few stools were unoccupied. Sitting on the one farthest from anyone else and leaning her forearms on the bar top, her eyes searched out the bartender.

An older man, maybe in his fifties, with graying hair and a slight paunch in his middle, stood behind the bar with his arms outstretched, hands resting against the nicked wood finish of the bar. He was talking to some burly men wearing grimy T-shirts and worn-out hats—though he surreptitiously glanced her way, letting Brooke know he'd seen her and was deliberately making her wait.

Finally, he seemed like he could be bothered enough to come over and talk to her. He dried his hands on a dingy towel that hung from his belt. "What can I do for ya?"

"Can I have the number for a local cab company?"

The man squinted one eye as he observed her. His appraisal was unsettling, to say the least. "You could. If we had such a thing here."

Brooke inhaled deeply as her eyes fluttered closed for a moment. It was like the gas station in Kansas all over again. It didn't say great things about where she was if there weren't even any cabs around. Everywhere had cabs. She looked back at the man who seemed to be enjoying her discomfort—if the smirk curling one side of his mouth was any indication. "Bus stop?"

The man nodded. "Bus runs through every day at eight."

She looked at her watch. It was only a little before seven. Surely she could deal with some seedy men for an hour. In her business, an hour trapped in a room with smarmy guys was considered catching a break. Slinging her backpack around and resting it on the bar, she said, "Okay, I guess I'll just wait here then. Do you have a menu?"

The man leaned closer as if he wanted to whisper a secret to her. She instinctively drew back, but that only made his smirk transform into a full-blown smile. And not a comforting one. "Can't wait here, miss. We close at two."

"But I thought you said the bus came at eight?"

"It does. Eight a.m."

Shit. "How far is the nearest motel?" She was almost afraid to hear his answer.

"About fifteen miles." The man backed off the counter and began rubbing his hands with the towel again, as if he was growing bored speaking to her.

Brooke felt at a loss, though she knew better than to show it. There was no way she could walk fifteen miles before dark set in. And being out on that empty stretch of road at night was *not* an option. She'd watched enough horror movies to know how that kind of thing worked out.

"Still want that menu?" the bartender asked, the mocking clear in his tone.

Brooke was thinking of how to answer when another voice spoke. "I can give ya a ride."

Turning slowly, Brooke was afraid to see which of the creatures had spoken.

"Hey, that's a good idea. Let Lyle give ya a ride," the bartender said. But his voice still held a sliver of sarcasm mixed with something else. Something scary. Like he was in on a joke she wasn't even aware had been told.

Brooke looked at Lyle. He appeared to be in his thirties and was built kind of how she'd imagine a crazy, backwoods lumberjack to be—tall, solid, scruffy, and creepy. This was the second stranger in two days who'd offered her a ride. But she knew immediately that she wouldn't accept this one. While Cole had been open and inviting, this man was dark and devious. "No thanks."

The man looked down at his boots and kicked at imaginary dirt before returning his leering gaze to hers. "Looks like you're outta other options."

"I'll think of something," she muttered before turning to face the bar. She felt Lyle move closer to her, the hairs all over her body rising. The bartender looked from Brooke to Lyle and then back to Brooke before walking to the other end of the bar to resume his conversation with the other men.

Brooke felt a piece of her hair being moved off her neck as Lyle leaned in. "If you'd rather wait for the bus, you could always spend the night in my truck. It's mighty comfortable."

Brooke consciously kept her breathing even and forced herself not to jerk away from Lyle's touch. Guys like him enjoyed games of cat and mouse. Brooke had no intention of playing. "Thanks for the offer. But I'm not interested." Brooke would call home before she'd leave the bar with this man. And that was saying something.

"Aw, you're starting to hurt my feelings, darlin'. I'm just trying to be nice."

Brooke turned and offered a small, tight smile. "I appreciate the offer. But I'll be fine. Thanks anyway." As she turned her face away from the man, she felt him press his body into her back—his erection undeniable against the top of her ass. He put his arms on either side of her, his hands lowering to the bar and caging her in.

She glanced down at the other end of the bar where the rest of the patrons sat. None of them looked her way.

"I'm going to offer one more time," he said into her ear, the heat of his breath making her flinch.

"Leave me alone. Please." She had to force herself to add the pleasantry at the end. Everything in her rebelled against offering this man anything that resembled begging, but she didn't know what else to do.

He ground himself into her. "I think we both know I'm not going to do that."

Brooke couldn't help the whimper that escaped her. She'd thought she already knew what fear felt like. She was wrong.

"Now you're going to get up and come with me to my truck without a fuss. You hear me?" The fake sweetness his voice had previously held had been replaced by scathing venom.

She swallowed past the lump of terror in her throat. "I'm not going to do that."

"Then I'll just have to make ya." His hands left the bar

suddenly and gripped her arms, pulling her back against him.

She struggled to break free of his grasp. "No. Please. Don't!"

"You deaf?" The question thundered through the bar, causing everything to grind to a halt. Lyle's hands didn't leave her, but they stopped pulling.

Her head whipped around toward the voice that sounded both gloriously familiar and intimidatingly new. *Cole.* He was there. And shit did he look furious.

"You say something to me, boy?" Lyle asked.

Cole's stature was calm as he leaned against a wall by the entrance. His posture made it seem like he had no opinion about what he was witnessing. But his clenched fists and the look in his eyes told a different story. "I asked if you were deaf. Seems to me the woman asked you to let her go." Cole pushed off the wall with his shoulder and stood up straight. "Your best bet is to listen."

Lyle released Brooke and stepped back, huffing out a small laugh as he did so. "That right?"

Cole nodded.

"And what if I don't?"

Cole took two steps closer. "Then this is going to get real ugly for you."

Brooke's eyes drifted to the other men at the bar. Cole was seriously outnumbered, which brought a whole new fear to the surface for her. The last thing she wanted was for Cole to get hurt protecting her. Especially when it was her fault they were in this mess in the first place. Luckily, while they looked interested in what was unfolding, none seemed inclined to intervene. At least not yet.

"I think you got that backwards," Lyle warned him.

Cole shrugged. "Come over here, and we'll find out."

Lyle snickered. "Wait right here, darlin'," he said to Brooke. "I'll be right back."

Lyle slowly advanced on Cole, who never moved. Brooke could see the coiled tension Cole was carrying in his shoulders. He was braced for a fight. And Brooke hoped it was one he could win.

Lyle took the last two steps to Cole quickly, cocking his arm back before swinging it forward. Cole sidestepped the punch with such grace and fluidity, it made Brooke wonder who she'd been sharing a truck with for the past day and a half. Cole turned, grabbing the arm Lyle had swung, and elbowed him hard in the face. Lyle staggered back, holding his nose as Brooke watched his blood drip to the floor.

Lyle lost all grace then, hurtling himself at Cole, who easily countered, somehow grabbing the man in a headlock, causing Lyle to lose his footing. When Cole released Lyle's neck so he could deliver a hard knee to Lyle's ribs, Brooke swore she heard the crunch of breaking bones. Cole pulled Lyle up by the hair and delivered two hard punches to the face, dropping him to the ground, where he remained.

When Cole stepped back, Brooke could see his clothing was slightly rumpled, his knuckles were bleeding, and a sheen of sweat blanketed his skin. He looked at Brooke. "Let's go."

Brooke quickly jumped off the stool, grabbed her bags, and headed for the exit. Cole didn't move until she was by the door, instead glaring at the other men in the bar as if daring them to make a move. They didn't. As Brooke held the door open for him, Cole casually made his way toward her.

Once outside, his pace picked up, and they almost sprinted to Cole's truck. But Brooke couldn't resist asking, "Where did you learn to fight like that?"

"Now's not a great time for questions. Get in the truck."

She did, throwing herself into the passenger seat and hugging her bag to her chest.

Cole put the key in the ignition and took off out of the parking lot and down the road.

The silence between them was charged with so many swirling emotions, Brooke could barely see through the haze of them. Not only had she pissed off the man beside her earlier, he'd then had to save her ass. She didn't deserve to have him come back for her, but she was infinitely grateful that he had. "Cole?"

"What, Brooke?" His words were clipped, residual anger flowing through them.

She flinched a little. The shock of what had almost happened to her continued to fray her almost spent nerves. "Thank you."

Cole let out a breath, his shoulders slumping with an exhale. It took him a second to speak, but he eventually did. "You're welcome, Princess."

She finally let herself relax and sink back into the seat, relief ghosting across her face. She'd never been happier to be somebody's princess.

CHAPTER FOUR

The adrenaline from the bar fight was still flowing through Cole as they drove along the deserted road. The sun had almost completely disappeared, causing the tall grass that covered the land as far as the eye could see to be swathed in burnt orange and red. It would have been beautiful if Cole had been capable of any fond thoughts in that moment.

Brooke sat silently in the seat beside him, feet up on the seat with her arms drawing her legs close to her body as though she were physically trying to hold herself together. The sight tore at him, but he was too swamped in negativity to talk to her yet.

Cole had never been happier to walk into a bar full of drunks in his life. God only fucking knew what would've happened to her if he hadn't shown up. Well, Cole likely did know, and the thought made him grip the steering wheel tighter.

Despite being thankful he was there, he also cursed himself for letting Brooke get into that situation in the first place. He should've tried harder to get her back in the truck instead of letting his temper get the best of him. At least his conscience hadn't abandoned him completely. When he'd driven away and come across the bar, he'd pulled into the parking lot and parked between two rigs so she wouldn't be able to see his truck. He hadn't quite figured out what he was going to do from there—whether he was going to try to convince her to ride with him again or follow her for a while like a creep—but none of that mattered as they drove down the mostly solitary road, save for a few farms here and there. She was safely seated beside him, and he was going to do his damnedest to make sure she stayed there.

Eventually they came to a small town with a motel, and Cole pulled into the lot. He was wired and could have driven farther, but he figured Brooke could use a break. "This okay?" he asked her as he threw the truck in neutral.

"Sure," she said softly before opening the door slowly and climbing out. She seemed to be moving on autopilot, which Cole couldn't blame her for.

She started pulling her bags out, but Cole stopped her. "I'll come back out for them after we get a room."

Nodding once, she turned and started toward the office. Cole followed a little behind her, trying to give her both space and assurance that he was there. A bell tinkled above them as they opened the door to the office. An older man walked out from the back and greeted them.

"Evening, folks. Looking for a room?" he asked.

"Please," Cole replied with a nod.

"One or two?" the man asked.

Cole looked at Brooke. He wanted whichever would make her more comfortable, but he had no idea if sharing a room with him would make her feel better or worse.

She looked back at him, her eyes glistening with what he

figured were either unshed tears or exhaustion. Or both. He maintained eye contact, willing her to know everything that was swirling around in his head. That he was sorry, both for being an asshole and for what she went through in the bar. That he wouldn't let anything else happen to her while she was with him. That she could trust him even though he'd almost let her down.

Finally, she closed her eyes for a few seconds before cutting her eyes to the man. "One room is fine."

"All we have left is rooms with one king bed. That okay with you all?"

"Yes, that's fine," Brooke replied.

The man rung them up and handed them keys, and Brooke paid. Cole walked her to their first-floor room and made sure she was safely inside before he ran out to grab their bags. He knocked when he returned and said a soft, "It's me."

The door opened quickly, and the way her eyes darted around spoke of her anxiety. He hurried inside, set their things down, and locked the deadbolt behind him.

Brooke picked up her bags, carried them to the dresser, and set them down on it before rummaging through them. Taking off his hat, Cole tossed it on a table before running his hands through his unruly hair.

"You want first dibs on the bathroom?" he offered. "You could relax for a bit, and I could see if there's anywhere to get food around here."

She whirled around to face him. "You're leaving?"

"I thought I'd see if anywhere would deliver first. If I do have to run out, I'll make sure to let you know before I go. Or I could wait and you could come with me."

He watched Brooke take a deep breath and lengthen her spine a little to reach her full height, which Cole guessed was at least a good six inches shorter than his own six-one.

"No, it's fine. I'll be fine with whichever you decide. We obviously need to eat. Oh, and here's some money for it," she said as she reached into her backpack, fished a few bills out, and extended them toward him. "This should cover it, right? How expensive can a pizza be? I'll just stay here. I'll be fine."

Cole took the money out of her hand, but that didn't stop her rambling.

"Maybe I'll take a bath. That's always relaxing. And I'll just wait here for you to get back."

"Brooke," Cole said softly. Her arms were crossed, and she was swaying slightly. Cole wanted to move toward her, but he didn't want to scare her.

"It's not like you'll be gone long. I'm sure there's a place to eat close by. So nothing to worry about. I can even pack my new duffel bag if you're gone for a while and I get bored. That'll keep me busy. Busy is good. Busy—"

Cole couldn't take it anymore. He took two steps forward and enveloped her in his arms.

She tensed for a second before she shuddered out a breath. He felt her body shake, but she made few sounds other than sniffling and a few sharp breaths. Smoothing his hands down her long hair, he shushed her and reassured her that it would be okay. That she was safe. That *he'd* keep her safe.

Eventually she settled and pulled away from him, rubbing her hands over her face. "God, I'm sorry. I cried all over your shirt."

"I don't care about the shirt."

She looked him in the eyes then and seemed to decide he was genuine because she gave him a small smile before stepping back even farther. She scanned the room before pointing at the table across from them. "There's a book over there. It may have some menus in it."

Sensing that she needed a little time to compose herself, Cole backed away and walked to the table to leaf through the book. "This place says they deliver 'til midnight. Were you serious about wanting pizza, or do you want somethin' else? They have all kinds of sandwiches."

"Pizza is fine."

"Okay. I'll give them a call. Did you... You probably have time for that bath if you want. I'll knock when it gets here."

She gave him another small smile as she nodded and gathered some clothes. Once she had her things, she walked toward the bathroom but hesitated with her hand on the knob. Without turning to face him, she said, "I know I already said thank you, but I feel like there aren't enough thank-yous in the world for what you did for me tonight. If you hadn't shown up, I don't even want to think about—"

"So don't," Cole interrupted. "Don't let your mind wander to what could've happened. Thinking like that'll make you scared of your own shadow before long."

"You're right. I'll try." And with that, she stepped into the bathroom and locked the door behind her.

♦ ♦ ♦ ♦

Brooke sank low into the bubbles and warm water that filled the tub. She couldn't even bring herself to care about when the tub had been scrubbed last. For now, she was content in her attempt to scald her body of the memories from the bar.

Cole was right. Thinking about what had almost happened—*would have* happened had he not shown up—wasn't going to help her. But she couldn't keep her mind from remembering the stale, smoky scent in the bar, the terrifying things that asshole had said to her, the hard clench of his hand on her arm. She grabbed a washcloth from the rack and scrubbed herself clean. She drained some of the soapy suds and turned on the tap so fresh, hot water refilled the tub. Brooke closed her eyes and tried to calm her breathing. It wasn't just the events of tonight. It was everything. Her temper, her stubbornness. She had to get a grip. Cole was going to leave her if she didn't stop acting like a lunatic.

Though she supposed that wasn't true. She'd given him an opportunity to leave once already, and he hadn't. *Thank God he hadn't.* There was no doubt in her mind all of the horrible things her mother had warned her about when Brooke had first taken off and called to let her parents know she hadn't been kidnapped would've come true had Cole not shown up.

"Fake it 'til you make it" was one of her mother's favorite phrases, and Brooke had become a master at it. Snark, sarcasm, and sharp wit were not just her trademark; they had become survival skills. Necessary in a business that allowed grown men to stare lasciviously at teenage girls under the guise of an "audition." Necessary in a world where parents cared more about social-media metrics than the well-being of their own child. She had vocal talent and yet for so long, no real voice of her own. But her attempt to find her own way, or at least step away for a moment to find herself...well, that had been humbling to say the least.

A soft rap on the bathroom door startled her, but her heart rate slowed when Cole's voice came through the door. "Pizza is here. No rush. I just wanted you to know."

Brooke inhaled and willed her voice to sound steady when she replied. "Okay. Thanks." She allowed herself to soak for a little while longer before climbing out, drying off, and getting dressed. She wrapped a towel around her hair and glanced in the mirror. She looked tired even though her body felt a little like a live wire. Unable to dredge up enough care to do anything about her appearance, Brooke opened the door and joined Cole.

He was lying back on the bed, one arm tucked behind his head as he clicked through channels. The pizza boxes sat unopened on the table. She wasn't sure why the fact that he'd waited for her to eat—that Southern charm making itself known again—made her eyes prickle, but she wasn't up for analyzing it either.

Cole sat up. "Hungry? It's still warm."

She gave him a small smile. "Yeah. Starving."

Returning her smile, Cole stood and opened the pizza boxes. "I wasn't sure what toppings you liked, so I got one with half sausage and half plain, and the other half pepperoni and half pineapple."

Brooke quirked an eyebrow. "Pineapple?"

Cole shrugged. "I thought it was somethin' a princess might order." Her eyes were drawn to his lips, which seemed to struggle against a smirk.

She let out a laugh, and the sensation rippled through her, chipping away at some of the rust that had felt stuck to her bones. "Do princesses like pineapple?"

Releasing a full laugh then, Cole said, "I honestly wasn't sure if you liked meat on your pizza, and it was the only other topping that came to mind. Though I'm thinkin' now that mushrooms or peppers would've been more normal."

"Well, as much as I hate to admit it, I do like pineapple on my pizza," she said as she walked over to the table and grabbed a slice. Glancing over at Cole, Brooke couldn't miss the satisfied look on his face. She bumped his shoulder. "You're really proud of your pizza-picking skills, aren't you?"

"You have no idea," he answered, causing them both to laugh again.

They settled on the bed with their slices on plates the pizza place had provided. A sitcom rerun played on the television. Other than getting up to get more pizza, both of them were quiet and still. Brooke realized she felt at ease with him. She felt like she'd known Cole much longer than two days. She'd trusted him almost from the beginning—at least as far as being confident he wouldn't harm her. But now that she knew he'd also defend her and was supremely qualified for such a task, whatever other walls she'd built up were beginning to crumble. She wasn't willing to tell him her life story, but she did want to know him beyond his being a passing body in her chaotic world. He'd made his way into her orbit, and despite the fact that she knew he'd be better off if she jettisoned him out into space, part of her—a big part—longed to keep him.

"So where'd you learn to fight like that?" Watching Cole handle himself earlier had been nothing short of amazing. While most of the fight was blurry in her memory, her fear cloaking it in fog, she did remember how adept he'd been. The fact that he could take down a man so easily should have made her uneasy, but it didn't. She instinctively knew Cole would never hurt her.

"Army," he said simply.

Brooke turned and appraised him. She could definitely see the soldier in him—his confident posture, the way he seemed to be alert even when he was relaxing. "How long did you serve?"

"Seven years. Just finished my last tour about nine months ago."

"You didn't want to make a career out of it?"

Cole looked down at his plate and toyed with his napkin. "Nope."

Brooke could tell there was a story there, but it was obvious he didn't want to share it. And while her curiosity was killing her, she also had things she didn't want to talk about, so she respected his privacy. "What's in Oregon?"

The way he sighed let her know this wasn't a better topic. "A buddy I met in the service."

"You thinking of moving out there with him?"

Something dark passed over Cole's face, but Brooke didn't know what it meant.

"That's not really an option. But I haven't ruled out settling down close by."

Brooke racked her brain for a topic that wouldn't make Cole seem so uncomfortable. "What do you do for work now that you're out of the army?"

Cole looked up at her. "I thought you didn't want to play Twenty Questions?"

He didn't look angry or irritated though, so she didn't let it deter her.

"I figured we'd be less likely to murder each other on the road if we knew each other better. But anything you don't want to tell me, just let me know, and I'll drop it."

"So we're travelin' together again?" The question sounded sincere, but it made Brooke fidget regardless.

"Uh, yeah? I thought we could, at least. Clearly I can't be trusted to be on my own," she said with a smile to hopefully make light of what had happened, even though it wasn't the least bit funny.

"It was as much my fault you were in that bar as yours. Nothin' that happened today made me think that you couldn't take care of yourself," he replied.

She inhaled deeply, knowing she didn't deserve his kindness and wanting to repay it in some way. "I never have," she said.

"Never have what?"

"I've never taken care of myself. Not really. And I wanted to prove I could, which is why I got out of your truck. But really it only reinforced what my parents have been saying to me for years."

"What do they say?" Cole's voice was quiet, but the sound of it echoed in her head.

She toyed with a frayed piece of the comforter as she replied. "That I'd be nowhere without them."

Cole inhaled sharply. "Sounds like your folks and my dad should hang out. They'd probably get on real well together."

"What does your dad say to you?"

"That I'm a bum who'll never amount to anything." Cole let out a humorless laugh. "Coming from the town drunk, it really shouldn't get to me the way it does."

They were quiet for a second before Brooke found the courage to say the words that felt like they were about to explode out of her chest. "For what it's worth, you're quite possibly the best guy I've ever met."

Rubbing the back of his neck with his hand, Cole looked almost pained. "I'm not sure whether that makes me really fucking happy or really fucking sad."

Brooke studied his face. "Why would it make you sad?"

"Because I'm nothin' special. And you deserve to be surrounded by guys who'll treat you well."

Unsure of what to say in response to the compliment, Brooke said the only truth she knew. "I think you're plenty special."

By silent agreement, they both turned back to the TV. A peacefulness washed over Brooke, and she sank into it so much that Cole clearing his throat startled her, though she tried not to show it. And Cole, bless him, didn't comment on it.

"We're going to be heading through some beautiful country over the next few days. Any interest in sightseeing along the way?" Cole asked.

She smiled at him. "I'd like that."

"Good." He stood and dropped his plate into the trash. "I'm gonna grab a shower. You okay out here for a bit?"

"Sure."

Cole shut himself in the bathroom, and she heard the shower turn on a moment later. Despite what had happened that day, Brooke considered herself lucky to have met Cole. After heading over to the closet, she grabbed two extra blankets that were stored there. She left one at the foot of the bed before lying on top of the comforter and covering herself with the other. She dropped the towel from her hair onto the floor beside the bed. Exhaustion threatened to pull her eyes closed, but she fought it. She wanted Cole to be next to her when she fell asleep.

He came out a little later, shirtless and in low-slung sweatpants. Approaching the bed, he looked hesitant. "I can take the couch if you want," he said as he gestured toward the small, tattered monstrosity across the room.

Brooke patted the space next to her in reply.

Cole didn't say anything else. He simply grabbed the spare blanket and lay down, leaving a large gap of space between them.

Brooke didn't want to overthink the fact that she nestled closer to him, practically burrowing into his side. He wrapped an arm around her and held her close.

"You can sleep, Princess. I got ya."

And because she knew he did, Brooke drifted off to sleep.

CHAPTER FIVE

Brooke hadn't slept that well for as long as she could remember. It was true she should be used to being on the road—though in nicer places than she'd stayed with Cole the past two nights—but there was something about having him beside her that allowed her to relax in a way she hadn't before. When she turned over to find he wasn't in bed anymore, she whipped her head to either side in search of him.

Before she could react further, she heard the toilet flush in the bathroom, followed by the sound of a razor turning on. She instantly relaxed, the realization that he was still here comforting her. Though she couldn't deny that part of her wanted him even closer. Cole soothed something inside of her. And while some of that had to be because of how he'd rescued her, some of it was also simply the man himself. Brooke felt herself opening up to him in ways that she might regret down the road, but damned if she felt like she could stop it from happening.

She knew she probably had at least a few minutes or so before Cole was done shaving, and that was more than enough time to give her sister a call and at least let her know she was okay.

Natasha picked up on the first ring. "Hey, Beck. What's

up?" Natasha asked, confusing the hell out of Brooke.

"What?"

"Did you see the video I posted last night of that squirrel?"

"What the hell are you talking about? What squirrel?" Brooke asked.

"Hang on. Let me go outside. The service in my kitchen's always spotty."

Brooke was about to ask her sister what the hell she was talking about, when she heard a door close on the other end of the line and her sister's voice drop to a whisper.

"You know it makes me seriously concerned for your well-being when you don't even realize that I'm trying to pretend you're someone else so Mom and Dad don't know I'm talking to you, right? How are you possibly surviving when you're so clueless?"

"Well hello to you too," Brooke replied dryly. "We just woke up a few minutes ago."

"We? You're still with that guy?"

"Yeah. We decided to travel together. He's heading to Oregon to visit a friend, and we could both use the company, so..." She let her sentence go unfinished, allowing her sister to draw her own conclusions about Brooke's decision, which she was sure was exactly what Natasha was doing.

"Are you sure that's the best idea?"

Natasha's question was a valid one, and Brooke knew she'd asked it only out of concern. "I don't know that it's the *best* idea. But I do know it's not the worst. I was on my own for a little yesterday, and..." When she felt her voice begin to shake, she tried to steady it, hoping like hell the person who knew her better than anyone wouldn't hear the shakiness. "I'm safer with him here," she said. "I trust him, Nat."

Natasha was quiet for a moment, her lack of protest a silent acceptance of Brooke's decision. "Just try not to get recognized, okay? Mom and Dad have been talking nonstop about how they can get you home as quickly as possible."

"Well, in that case, I should probably cancel our plans for karaoke later."

"Stop," Natasha said. "That's not funny."

"It's a little funny," Brooke replied, glad to have a light moment. "I mean, could you picture me singing some of my own songs at a crowded bar?"

"I don't want to picture that, and neither should you. I'm surprised no one's recognized you yet."

That same thought had crossed Brooke's mind on more than a few occasions, but the truth was, neither her name nor her appearance were recognizable to most of the country. At least not *yet*. "That's why I left, Nat. At least right now I still have some sort of privacy. If I become a household name, any chance I have at a normal life will be gone." She heard her voice get softer, sadder as she spoke. "I never wanted any of this." When she heard the razor turn off, her eyes darted to the bathroom. "I gotta go. Cole's probably almost done in the bathroom. He'll be out any second."

"You're sharing a room with him?"

"It's a long story."

"There's a *story*?"

Brooke rolled her eyes but then smiled. It was a good thing her sister couldn't see it. "Goodbye, Natasha."

"Bye, Brookey. Call again soon, okay?"

"As soon as I can," Brooke answered. She hung up and stared at the ceiling as the conversation with Natasha echoed in her mind. Part of Brooke wondered if she should tell Cole who she was. It might make her seem less like a criminal on the lam if she came clean about her music career. Not that it was much of a career at this point, but if her parents had their way, she'd go from relatively unknown to a household name in a matter of months.

But she couldn't bring herself to do it. At least not yet. She liked that Cole didn't pull any punches with her. He was real in a way very few people had ever been with her, and she didn't want to lose it. Especially not when she was already feeling so vulnerable.

She decided it could wait just as Cole emerged from the bathroom. She did her best not to stare at his exposed chest, but it was impossible. Since she was still on the bed, her face was basically below crotch-level, making it difficult for her to look at his face without her eyes first scanning up his body.

"You're up. I hope I didn't wake you," he said, walking over to his bag and crouching down to find some fresh clothes. She scooted up the bed so she was resting against the headboard as she watched him. The muscles in his back flexed as he dug around in his bag. Then he stood, turning around to face her. When he pulled a white T-shirt over his head to cover his chest—which she'd noticed had short blond hairs on it—and chiseled abs, her brain began working again, reminding her that she should probably speak.

"No. No, you didn't."

"Good. You needed the rest. Did you sleep okay last night?"

"Yeah. I slept well, actually." She said it like she was surprised, but the truth was, having Cole close to her made her feel protected, safe. "How 'bout you?"

"Pretty good," he answered as he walked back into the bathroom, partially closing the door.

She was sure he didn't realize his reflection was visible to her in the vanity mirror right outside of the bathroom, making it impossible for her not to watch as he dropped the pants he'd slept in and pulled on his tight boxers and dark khaki shorts. Though she only caught a glimpse of the side of his round ass, it was enough to make her think about what it would feel like in her hands as he moved inside her. *This is not what you should be thinking about right now.*

"Bathroom's all yours whenever you're ready. No rush, though. I thought we could stay one more night here if that's okay with you. It'd give us the day to relax. I'm pretty sure we're in Oklahoma, and I wouldn't mind seeing what there is to do around here. I mean, it's no Georgia," he said with a smile. "But I'm sure there's somethin' fun to do."

"Sure. Yeah, that'd be good."

"All right then," he said with a nod. "You mind if I run down to the office and talk to them about staying another night? I'll pick up a map or something."

Her first instinct was to tell him not to go, that she didn't want to be here without him. But she realized how ridiculous that would sound. He was only going a few doors down to the office and would be back in a couple of minutes. "Yeah, that's fine," she answered. Then she got up and headed over to the pile of stuff she'd bought at the mall yesterday. "I'll get a shower while you're gone, and then we can decide what to do."

"Sounds good," Cole said before throwing on a hat and leaving the room, thankfully not questioning why she'd need another shower when she'd taken a bath the night before.

◆ ◆ ◆ ◆

Cole did his best to be quick. He spoke to the woman in the office, booked the room for a second night, and then talked to her for a minute or so about the area's attractions, which weren't many. Though Brooke had said she didn't mind him leaving, the hesitation in her voice and the way her eyes darted to the floor had told him otherwise. It made sense, given her experience at the bar the previous night, but since this wasn't the first time Brooke had seemed nervous to be alone, it made him wonder what exactly she was scared of. But he knew better than to ask.

His curiosity increased when he returned to the room and unlocked the door, only to find that she'd locked the chain after he'd left. Whether she'd forgotten he wouldn't be able to get back in or was just too freaked out to care, he wasn't sure. But he figured either way she'd be out of the bathroom soon enough. Until then, he'd lean against the motel's stucco exterior and study the map he'd picked up so he could mentally plot out a possible route to Oregon.

About fifteen minutes later, Cole knocked on the door. He didn't want to startle her by opening it, even if the chain prevented him from coming in. "It's me," he called after knocking. "You out of the shower yet?" He didn't hear an answer, but a few seconds later, he heard the slide of metal and then the door opened.

"Sorry," she said. "Force of habit. I always use the security latch or deadbolt or whatever."

"You travel a lot?"

"Yeah. More than I'd like to," she said. "What about you?"

"Never really went anywhere at all until I enlisted." He didn't want to expand on his statement since the obvious follow-up would've been to tell her where he'd been and what he'd seen. Neither of which he wanted to discuss with her. Or with anyone, for that matter. So his best bet was to change the subject. "Speaking of traveling"—he held up the map—"I think I got an idea of a route we could take on our way to Oregon."

"Oh yeah?"

He opened the map back up but held it over his head when Brooke came over and tried to pull her side of it down so she could see what he was looking at. "No way, Princess. Just so we're clear, this map is for looking only. No touching."

"Very funny," she said with a pout that made her lips look even plumper than they already did.

He suddenly felt a desire to kiss them. A desire he'd need to keep in check. "I'm not kidding," he added dryly. "The last time you were in charge of a map didn't end too good, so I'm takin' control of this one."

She crossed her arms and rolled her eyes at him, but her exaggerated huff told him she wasn't as annoyed with him as she let on. "Fine. Where are we going, Thelma?"

He raised an eyebrow at her. "Thelma?"

"Yeah. Like *Thelma and Louise*."

"But Louise is the driver in that movie."

"Whatever. I saw that movie like a million years ago. And Thelma's the weirder name, so that's what I'm calling you." She gave him a smile. "As long as I'm Princess, you're Thelma," she said.

This time he was the one rolling his eyes. "You wanna know where I think we should go, or not?"

"Yes, I want to know. That's why I tried to grab the map."

He shook his head at her before sitting down on the bed with the map. Immediately, she was at his side, watching his finger trace their possible path across the country. "I think we should head through Colorado next," he said. "And then Utah. But after that, we could do either Idaho or Nevada." He lifted his head so he could look at her. "You have a preference?"

"I don't know. I guess it depends what there is to do in each and what we plan to do in Colorado and Utah. Did you have any ideas? Anything you were planning to see before you decided to pick up some crazy brunette?"

After being in a car and hotel rooms for so long, Cole wanted nothing more than the fresh, open air that states like those offered. But Brooke didn't strike him as the type to go hiking or kayaking or anything like that, so he needed to introduce the idea subtly. "I've always wanted to see the Rockies. Driving through Colorado without seein' 'em doesn't seem right." He was aware that his argument was weak, but truthfully, until the two of them had decided to travel together, his only focus had been on getting to Oregon.

"Okay, so this is probably a dumb question, but what do

you actually *do* in the Rockies? Do you just look at them?"

Cole tried to stop the laugh that threatened to burst from him but failed miserably.

"Don't laugh at me," she said with a swat to his bicep. "I told you it was probably a dumb question. I'm more of a city girl. I don't have a whole lot of experience with this type of thing."

"You don't say," he teased. "I figured you for one of those people who can find their way around by the stars. Thought that was maybe why you threw the map away."

"Are you ever gonna let me live that down?"

"Probably not." Once Cole was able to get his laughter under control, he spoke again. "Okay, okay," he said. "Guess it's a fair enough question. And to answer it, there's a ton to do in the Rockies, even in the summer. Hiking, horseback riding, boating. Like in a kayak or canoe or something. It wouldn't be like a yacht or anything," he added quickly, making Brooke roll her eyes at him.

"I'm familiar with boats that aren't yachts."

"What? Like a cruise ship?"

"Shut up," she said, playfully pushing her shoulder into his. But instead of pulling back afterward, her body remained against his. "But seriously, those things do sound like fun. I could use the exercise, and I'd probably never do any of those things if I weren't with you."

Cole thought about telling her that his thoughts mirrored hers exactly, but he thought better of it because their reasons for feeling that way were vastly different. Instead, he simply said, "Sounds good," before they moved on to talk about the other states. Surprisingly, Brooke said she'd rather go through Idaho than Nevada because she said she'd already been to Vegas a few times. And though he hadn't been there himself, he didn't think he would be missing much.

Brooke seemed to like the idea of seeing nature more than he'd expected her to, so he suggested they stop at some of the national parks along the way.

Her eyes rose from the map and settled on his. There was a seriousness to her stare that made him wonder what she was about to say. "I should've asked this earlier, but we're not gonna be camping, are we? Because I draw the line at sleeping with bears."

Cole chuckled at her vision of what camping would be like but chose not to correct her. "No, Princess. Tents don't have mirrors, so I figured you'd wanna stick with hotels."

"Then I'm in," she said. "But just for the record, Thelma. You're way prettier than I am."

CHAPTER SIX

Trying to decide what the best deal was, Cole stepped back to read the sign again that had the ticket prices and cost of a bracelet, which would let them go on unlimited rides. "So how does this work exactly?" Cole asked the woman at the carnival ticket booth.

"Just what the sign says, hon. Twenty-five dollars for a bracelet or twenty for a strip of twenty-two tickets."

"How many tickets are the rides?"

"Depends on what you plan on ridin'." She raised one of her thin, painted eyebrows at him like his question was a dumb one. "This your first fair?"

"No," he answered with a laugh he worried revealed his embarrassment. "Just wonderin' if the bracelet's worth it."

Before the woman could speak, Brooke stepped closer to the booth. She'd been off to the side slightly, but now she was pushing Cole aside with her small body and handing the woman fifty bucks. "We'll take two bracelets," she said.

The woman took the money before handing the bracelets to Brooke and telling them to have a good time.

"I would've paid for those," Cole said as they walked toward some of the rides. "It was my idea to come here."

"Well, there was a group of teenage girls behind you who

were murdering you with their eyes, so I thought we should speed it up."

Cole let out a sharp laugh. "I ain't afraid of no girls," he joked.

Brooke put on her red-and-white-paper bracelet. Then she looked around at her surroundings, which made Cole do the same. The fair was much bigger than the ones he'd been to in Georgia growing up. While the ones he'd been used to had been held in a small field or a high school parking lot, this one had to be acres. He wasn't sure how long it had been going on, but the grass had been worn down to a dirt path by all of the foot traffic. Cole hadn't been around this many people in... Well, he preferred not to think about things he'd seen overseas. This was a completely different situation in a completely different country. And the small children that ran by his hip as he walked were no doubt running *toward* something, rather than away from it.

Inhaling deeply, he tried to focus on the comforting smell of funnel cake and some sort of barbecue he knew he'd be eating before he left this place. The scents comforted him as he pulled out his hat from where it had been shoved into his back pocket and put it on his head to block out the sun. He had to admit—though only to himself—the prospect of getting on some of these contraptions scared the hell out of him. He'd never been a fan of traveling fairs like this, where the rides were disassembled and reassembled so frequently. All it took was one loose screw to send the riders plummeting to their deaths. "So what do you wanna ride first?" he asked, almost laughing out loud at the forced enthusiasm.

"Whatever. I'll go on almost anything," Brooke said. Her excitement was evident in the way she bounced on her toes, as if she couldn't keep the emotion inside her. It was endearing. "And we can do everything eventually, multiple times if we want."

That was *not* the answer Cole was hoping to hear, but he managed to smile anyway and say, "Sounds great."

"You want to do that one?" Brooke pointed at some ride that was shaped like an oblong Ferris wheel with enclosed metal boxes for people to sit.

Cole watched them flip around as the oval wheel spun, and he said a silent prayer before answering, "Sure."

A few minutes later, they were belted into the seat, peering out through the holes in the chipped yellow metal. At least if the thing fell off during the ride, the cage would hopefully break their fall. "You can hold my hand," he said. "If you get scared, I mean."

"I'll probably be good," she replied. "But thanks. Last time I was at Disney, I went on the Tower of Terror three times. I would've done it more, but I'd used my fast passes, and the line was long."

"How many times have you been there?" he asked as they waited for the ride to start.

She thought for a moment. "Maybe seven or so."

"Jesus. You really *are* a princess. Did little kids line up to get their pictures with you?"

"No," she answered almost immediately. "Why would they do that?"

The defensiveness to her question made him wonder

if he'd actually offended her. "Because Disney made you an honorary princess," he explained slowly. "It was a joke. Though I guess not a very good one."

"Oh" was all she said as they sat there waiting. Then Brooke spoke again. "There are some things about me I'd really rather not talk about. But I don't mean to be mysterious."

Cole turned toward her so she'd know he was listening, but he didn't respond, deciding to wait and see if she wanted to say more.

"I told you a little about my family. Can we just say that a lot of my trips there weren't so that I could go on the rides and we'll leave it at that?"

"We can leave it at whatever you want, Princess."

She seemed to relax, and then the ride started, and the need for words disappeared in the wind that blew in their faces.

Cole managed to survive, though barely. It had been years since he'd been on any sort of a ride that went upside down like that, and his stomach turned from all of the jerking and flipping. Over the next twenty minutes or so, they went on a few more rides—a small roller coaster, the Ferris wheel, and one of those boat things that swings back and forth in the air. Brooke whooped and hollered, threw her hands in the air, and smiled like she had found her own happiest place on earth. Cole had his eyes closed for most of them while he prayed the mechanics didn't fail and he wouldn't throw up. The fact that his prayers had been answered made him not want to press his luck by going on anything else right now. "You wanna watch that competition?" he asked, nodding to where several people had gathered on a small stage. "They have to identify livestock and crops and stuff. Things like this were huge in my town when I was growing up. It says there's a seven-year-old competing."

"Sure," Brooke said. "As long as we can play some games before we leave."

Cole liked the way that sounded. "Deal."

They watched the competition—Brooke much more into it than he would've guessed—before they moved on to the games. They started at one that involved tossing rings onto beer bottles, but neither of them could get any on after three games, so they called it quits. Then Brooke insisted that she could "definitely" win a stuffed animal at one of those huge claw games. "No way," Cole told her. "The claw doesn't close until it's too far up to grab anything. Those things are rigged."

"That's a loser's mentality," she said, not even bothering to look back at him as she pulled him in the direction of the claw machine she'd spotted about ten yards away.

"Did you just call me a loser?" he asked, pretending to be insulted.

"Shut up and watch how this is done."

When they arrived at the giant claw—which held stuffed animals Cole was sure could be purchased from any Walmart for a fraction of what Brooke was probably about to feed this machine—she immediately unzipped her bag and pulled out a ten-dollar bill. Cole watched her as she studied the people in front of her play a few more games before eventually giving up. "So what's your strategy here?" he asked.

"Not sure yet. But I'm thinking I'm not gonna go for the obvious ones. That's what the machine wants, but I'm not falling for it."

ELIZABETH HAYLEY

Cole laughed, but he did think her theory had some validity to it.

"I also think it's probably a bad idea to actually go for one right away. Maybe moving one or two around will be better."

"Right. Focus on the long game, Princess. Show that machine who's boss." Standing next to her, he lifted his arms over his head and rested them on the top of the machine as she fed the money into the slot.

She tried unsuccessfully a few times to move a blue dog that was flipped upside down, but the claw kept sliding off the leg before it was able to move it more than an inch or so. Then she moved on to a pink rabbit and was able to take hold of its ear enough to dislodge it from its place between the other animals.

Brooke was singularly focused on the stuffed animals, but Cole was focused on her. The way she'd poke her tongue out of the corner of her mouth as she concentrated, the way she'd jump up and down slightly when the crane dropped. She was so...appealing to him. As rough around the edges as she could be sometimes, there was a pureness to her enjoyment that made him want to do more things that would make her this happy.

She spent a total of twenty dollars before evidently deciding it wasn't worth the effort anymore. "Okay, I give up. You're right. This thing's rigged," she said, making Cole smile.

"I'm gonna play one game," he said. "I hate these things, but I can't leave without trying."

"Be my guest," she said before stepping aside so he could take over.

79

He slid two dollars into the machine and moved the claw toward the pink bunny. Both times, the claw did the same for him as it'd done for her, leaving him with nothing. "Okay, I'm done. Looks like I'm a loser after all," he joked, though the truth to his words wasn't lost on him.

Brooke shrugged. "Guess we're both losers." Then a smile overtook her face. "Maybe, in our case, two losers can make a winner."

Cole returned her smile. "I like the sound of that."

They looked at one another for a beat, and Cole could feel the chemistry crackling between them. Though neither seemed inclined to break it, finally Brooke did.

"It's getting late. Want to get outta here?"

"Sure," he replied.

They walked toward the exit, their arms brushing against each other's. But before they left, Cole spotted one of those games where each player squirts a water gun at a target. "Let's do this one before we go," he said. "It's more my speed. Plus, if we wait until those kids are done, one of us will definitely win something because we'll be the only ones playing."

They waited a few steps behind the two girls who were playing and watched as the small children, who looked no older than seven or eight, tried to find the target with the stream of water. Finally, the older girl won, and she was handed a giant stuffed snake. When she started to complain that she wanted something else, her father tried to console her while still explaining she needed to stop or they'd be leaving.

As he ushered the two girls away from the game, the man froze at the sight of Brooke and Cole, though Cole had no idea why. They weren't close enough to have startled them, and the family's eyes stayed fixed on them—or on Brooke rather—without making any attempt to move.

"Can I help you?" Cole asked, infusing his voice with enough assertiveness to hopefully get this guy to snap out of whatever the fuck was his problem.

"Sorry," the man said with a shake of his head. The older girl looked at Brooke and then up at her father. Her little sister seemed to be oblivious to whatever her sister and dad were staring at. "You look like someone."

Cole looked to Brooke, who was visibly shaken. Her face had turned almost completely white, and though her mouth was open slightly, no sound was coming out of it. "I'm not," Brooke finally said.

"I know," the man replied as he pressed his young girls against his sides. "You're not... You look like my wife," he said, shaking his head again like the action might make the image in front of him disappear. "But she passed three years ago."

Cole inhaled deeply and let his broad shoulders relax a bit. When he looked at Brooke, the color seemed to be returning to her face, though she still seemed out of sorts. "I'm sorry," Cole said.

The man gave a tight-lipped grin. It was one of those actions that people force to make them seem like they're okay when they're anything but. Cole was intimately familiar with that smile. "Cancer," the man added. "I apologize for staring like that," he said to Brooke. "I can tell I scared you. But Jesus, you look so much like her. The same features, hair, everything. It's like looking at a ghost."

"It's okay," Brooke said. "I'm so sorry about your wife."

"Thank you." He rubbed his girls' shoulders as he seemed to realize his daughters were as freaked as Brooke was, if not more. "We should get going. Enjoy the fair," he said before walking briskly away with his girls.

"That was...intense," Brooke said once they were a safe distance away.

"Yeah," Cole answered. Though he couldn't help but think the only thing weirder than that guy's reaction to Brooke was *her* reaction to him.

◆ ◆ ◆ ◆

Stepping out of the shower, Brooke finished drying off and then turned toward the bathroom mirror, bracing her hands against the worn beige vanity as if the fixture's physical stability might provide her with some emotional support as well. She took a deep breath, letting the steam from her shower invade her nostrils. Finally, she was able to find enough courage to wipe the fog from the mirror so she could see her reflection.

It was the first time in her life she'd ever been anything but a brunette, and she wasn't sure she liked the change. Though she guessed it didn't matter. Because what she was pretty sure she'd hate more than her new hair was someone recognizing her. The guy at the fair had spooked her. And it was enough to make her do almost anything to ensure she could travel the rest of the way to...wherever it was she was going without getting discovered.

When they'd left the carnival, Brooke had asked Cole to stop at a drugstore, but she hadn't told him why. Not that he'd asked. She was sure he probably thought the bag she'd returned with held tampons or something he didn't care to know about instead of hair dye, scissors, a handheld mirror, and shampoo and conditioner specifically formulated for blondes. She'd figured it would help keep the unnatural color in as long as possible over her dark hair.

She'd left the dye in for twice as long as the box suggested, hoping to make her hair as light as possible with the store-bought product. But it still had darker shades in some spots, though it didn't exactly look *bad*. Just...different. And as she lifted the scissors up to her hair, which hadn't been above her shoulders since second grade, she told herself different was good. It was what she needed. Change was the reason she'd left Philadelphia to begin with. It had occurred to her multiple times on the drive back to the hotel that she had no idea how to cut hair. But she figured if she screwed it up, she could always stop at a cheap salon somewhere to get it touched up. She was all but positive no one would recognize her once her hair was blond *and* short.

Standing in front of the mirror, she did her best to give herself a textured cut that she hoped resembled Cersei Lannister and not Brigitte Nielsen as whatever her name was in the fourth *Rocky* movie. Brooke was conservative at first, trimming small pieces here and there, until she grew accustomed to the shorter length. Eventually she ended up with what she felt was the best she could do under the circumstances—some sort of combination between an asymmetrical bob and a long pixie cut. And surprisingly she didn't think it would look half bad with a little product on the ends.

She pulled gently at her hair, which was so thick it still hadn't dried completely, even though she didn't have much left. Once she brushed the hair off herself and cleaned up the bathroom a bit, she put on a white tank top and navy cotton shorts before opening the door cautiously. She wasn't sure why she was nervous for Cole to see her. She didn't have to look *good*. She just had to look like someone other than herself. But not having to have it didn't mean she didn't want it. Cole had slipped past her defenses and become important to her, and his opinion mattered. A lot.

She took her time moving far enough into the room that her presence caught Cole's eye, causing him to avert his gaze from whatever he'd been watching on TV to her. His eyes widened in a way that made her want to run into the bathroom and glue all the discarded strands of hair back on her head. "Does it look that bad?"

"No," he said with a small shake of his head. His words seemed to catch in his throat after inhaling a sharp breath. "That...*good*." He moved to a sitting position on the bed, letting his long legs hang over the side as he squared himself to her. "I've never been that into women with short hair, but you may have just changed that."

His admission made her smile shyly.

"What made you...? Why did you...? I mean, it looks amazing. Really. Really fucking amazing, but—"

"I needed a change." She ran a hand through what was left of her hair, feeling oddly naked without it.

Cole's lips lifted into a subtle smile, but it looked more

out of desire than happiness. "Change is good," he said, and the rasp to his voice had all the nerve endings in her body prickling under her skin.

There was a silent moment, but somehow even without the words, Brooke was sure Cole felt the same thing she did. There had been something growing between them that Brooke could without a doubt identify as attraction—both sexual and emotional. Their eyes stayed fixed on the other's, neither of them willing to initiate what Brooke knew both of them wanted. The air between them seemed to thicken with every passing second, and Brooke was suddenly aware of the crackle, like a fire about to fully ignite. She felt an ache between her legs that was building quickly, so quickly that the sensation was as surprising as it was enjoyable.

She hadn't been expecting Cole to touch her when he did, but suddenly his hands were on hers, pulling her toward him with one firm movement. He paused for a moment, Brooke guessed, to see if it was okay. Her hand moved through his hair as her silent concession, and when she pulled his face toward her, she knew there was nothing more she wanted than his hands and lips all over her. He kissed her stomach after lifting her shirt up enough to give him access. The feeling had her legs growing limp beneath her. Her pelvis drew toward him while his strong, rough hands rubbed over her legs and under her shorts to her ass, which was flexing with her need for him.

Slowly, his mouth moved lower. He began tugging at the waistband of her shorts as the pressure built inside her. He dragged her shorts and underwear down until they dropped at her feet, and she was able to step out of them.

She didn't even care she was standing in front of this guy, who was all but a complete stranger, naked from the waist down. Her body overrode the part of her brain that told her this probably wasn't a good idea. The thought was only a small flicker in her mind, and one that died fast. There was no way she could resist him, resist *this*. No way she could tell him to stop what he'd started. Not when he'd made her this wet with only a few strokes of his hands over her skin. She needed a release any way she could get it.

Guiding him back a bit, she pulled his shirt over his head and tossed it to the side. And then she was on him, shamelessly straddling him as she removed her own shirt. She hadn't put on a bra after her shower, and Cole's fingers immediately went to her nipples, tugging and pinching to the point just before pain. It was rough and carnal, and she couldn't imagine anything she wanted more at the moment.

Except for maybe his cock, which she could feel hard against his jeans as she rubbed over him. She was sure she could come from this, *would* come from this, if she kept grinding against him. And his low groans and sharp breaths told her he could probably do the same. But it wasn't enough. She wanted more. She wanted it all.

"Please, Cole."

"Take what you want, Brooke."

He was giving her control, and she adored him for it. "Do you have any condoms?" she asked.

"Yeah," Cole said on a short exhale. "Hang on." He rolled her over and stood to walk toward his bag. A few seconds later, he was back, his hands unbuttoning the worn denim and dragging the zipper down. It was a kind of strip tease she was sure hadn't been intentional. But God, was it hot.

When his cock sprang free after removing his tight boxers, she inhaled deeply and imagined what it was going to feel like to have it inside her. Like Cole, it was long and solid, and watching him sheath himself with the slick latex did things to her she hadn't experienced before.

He kissed her deeply again. The connection was raw and consuming, and Brooke couldn't get enough of it. She wrapped her legs around his hips as she silently begged him to enter her. When he finally pushed inside, the feeling was intoxicating. The fullness had the pressure deep within her building with every drive of his hips.

There was no slow climb toward orgasm, no gradual build toward the release they both needed. Their movements were rushed and wild—warm skin against warm skin, lips nipping hungrily at damp flesh, heavy breaths muffling an occasional curse word. It was a frantic connection between two people who seemed to need exactly that.

There was no warning when Brooke finally felt her climax shoot through her like a tidal wave before it ebbed gently and eventually tapered off completely. So lost in her own afterglow, she was barely aware when Cole found his own release. He pumped into her a few more times as he whispered a soft "Fuck." And then, "That was intense."

He hovered above her for a few seconds, bearing most of his weight on his arms, until he pulled out slowly and rolled over next to her. She wasn't sure why, but she expected him to get up immediately and throw away the condom, but he pulled the sheet up just to his hipbone and let his head flop to the side so he could look at her.

When she allowed her own face to turn toward his, her eyes locked on his green ones as she uttered the only words that came to mind. "It really was."

It was one of the most honest things she'd said to him since they'd met.

CHAPTER SEVEN

Brooke refused to open her eyes even though she could feel the heat of the sunlight warming her face. She was afraid if she let herself wake up all the way, she'd find that the large, warm body spooning against her was a dream. And as much as her life was already a complicated mess without adding a crush on a virtual stranger into the mix, there was something about Cole that made her want to burrow into him and stay there. So she did. Shifting herself back a little, she pressed her back more firmly into his chest, causing his arm to tighten around her.

He pulled her even closer, which made his morning erection push into the back of her thigh. She squirmed lower on the bed so it pressed against the meat of her ass, and then she rocked backward.

A soft moan escaped Cole as his hand drifted down to her hip. "You're trouble," he murmured.

The poor guy had no idea. "I thought you'd like this kind of trouble."

He gyrated against her slowly. "I do."

They'd never gotten dressed from the previous night, so all it took was Cole grabbing a condom off the bedside table, lifting her leg slightly, and pushing his sheathed and throbbing length into her.

"Jesus," she moaned. Her fingers clutched the pillow as the euphoric feeling of being fucked by Cole's long, thick cock spread throughout her body.

"Name's Cole, but I *am* fond of nicknames," he whispered in her ear.

She could feel his smile against her neck, which made her own lips tilt up for a second before a moan wiped it away.

Cole's fingers dipped down to her clit and stroked her with soft, repetitive swirls that were driving her crazy with lust. It was enough to make her buck with ecstasy but not enough to make her orgasm.

"Cole, please... I need—"

"I know. I'll get you there."

"Get me there faster."

The bastard chuckled. "No."

But his thrusts did pick up speed, though the movement of his finger never changed. She tried grinding against him to increase the contact, but Cole's strong hand was able to hold her thigh in place against him while his finger kept up its ministrations.

"You seem a little desperate, Princess."

"Shut up and fuck me like you mean it."

He nipped her earlobe, the hint of pain ratcheting up her pleasure even higher. "Such language," he scolded. But he complied as he thrust into her with fast, deep strokes. He rubbed her clit with quicker, firmer movements, and she felt herself slowly falling apart under his attention.

Her release slammed into her hard, the waves of her

orgasm flowing through her core and making their way through every inch of her body. He continued fucking her through it, driving in forcefully like no matter how deep he got, it would never be far enough. It drew her pleasure out as her body convulsed. She felt like a towel being wrung dry. Every time she thought she had nothing left to give, a little more pleasure poured out of her.

Cole pushed into her one final time, a guttural groan leaving him as he quivered with his own release. He let his forehead rest against the back of her hair as they both regained their breaths. After a few moments, he pulled out and got up to dispose of the condom. He returned quickly and slid back into bed behind her, pulling her closer. She loved how it felt being wrapped in his arms. Part of her thought she could become addicted to it if she wasn't careful. A bigger part didn't want to be careful. Because she wasn't just wrapped up in Cole physically. The things she was starting to feel for him went much deeper than that. But not knowing exactly how he felt kept her from expressing any of that out loud.

"If you'd told me you could fuck like that, I wouldn't have been so hesitant to get into your truck that first day," she joked. She felt, more than heard, him laugh.

"I'll keep that in mind the next time I encounter a woman stranded at a gas station."

"I'm sure it will put her immediately at ease." As much as Brooke wanted to bask in the afterglow, she knew they didn't have all day to lie around. "What time is it?"

"Almost ten."

"What time is checkout?"

"Eleven."

She let out an exaggerated groan. "I don't wanna get up."

"Then don't. We've got some time." He pulled her closer, nuzzling into her shoulder and then kissing her neck in a way that made Brooke's body light up with pleasure again.

Cole drifted his hand down her stomach, and his cock was hard again against her ass. He ground against her a bit before slowing his movements and then whispering that they should probably get up if they didn't want to be charged for another day.

Brooke wanted to tell him she didn't give a shit if the motel charged them for another month if it meant Cole's cock could be inside her again, but she decided instead on, "Later then?" To which he enthusiastically agreed.

A few moments later, Brooke finally pulled herself up and stretched. "I guess I'll get ready." It might have been the least excited she'd been to do anything in her life.

"Well, at least your prep time has been cut down now that you hacked all your hair off," Cole teased.

Brooke ran a hand through her shorter locks. "You sure it looks okay?"

Studying her, Cole squinted a little and wobbled his hand as if to say it was so-so.

Reaching over, she smacked him on the stomach, which caused his abs to tighten. The army had definitely done Cole's body good. The definition of the phrase "rock-hard abs."

He bolted up and wrapped his arms around her before pulling her down on top of him. "I'm kiddin'. You look beautiful. Though you looked beautiful before that too."

"You're just saying that so you keep getting laid on this trip." She'd meant the words as a joke, but his expression was serious.

"Is that somethin' we should talk about?"

"What needs to be said about it?"

"I just... Eventually we're going to have to go our separate ways. I want to make sure that when that time comes, we don't leave on a bad note."

Brooke couldn't help the smirk that took over her lips. "Is this your way of telling me not to get attached?"

"It's not... I don't... God, you're a pain in the ass. I want to make sure I don't do anything to hurt you, okay? Now that we've reached a truce of sorts, I don't want to fuck it up."

"So, you're saying I should stop planning what flowers we should have at our wedding?"

He grabbed a pillow and hit her with it. "You drive me crazy."

"See? All the trappings of a great wife already." He groaned at her, which made her laugh. "I'm kidding. I know where you're coming from, and I agree. I'm in no place for anything permanent, so we're on the same page. But I also don't want to act like I'm not going to jump your bones for the rest of this trip. So let's enjoy it, and when it's time to say our goodbyes, we'll do so without drama. Deal?"

He studied her for a second, maybe trying to determine the sincerity of her words. But she did mean them. Eventually she would have to go home and figure out what her next steps would be. There was no way she could handle a relationship at the same time she faced the wrath of her parents and determined what she wanted from her future. This trip was a frozen moment of time for her. In a few weeks, her life would have to start moving again. But she planned to live the hell out of the moment until then.

Cole must have heard what he needed because he replied, "Deal."

"Good." She pressed a chaste kiss to his cheek before scooting off him and getting up. "I'm going to grab another shower."

"Need help reachin' your back?" he said.

"No, but there are a few other areas that could use your attention."

Cole leaped from the bed. "Lead the way, Princess."

Brooke ignored how much she was starting to like the nickname as she led him into the bathroom and had the dirtiest shower of her life.

♦ ♦ ♦ ♦

A few hours later, they'd checked out, gotten a quick bite to eat at a diner, and were on the road driving into Colorado. They'd made idle chitchat so far, making comments on the scenery as they passed it, but nothing of any depth. For some reason, the fact that they both seemed to skirt personal questions began to grate on Cole. It was like they were both treading carefully, afraid of setting off a landmine in someone's past. They'd been traveling for a bit now, and while he didn't want to share his entire life story with Brooke, he did want them to know each other beyond what they looked like naked.

"So you said you've traveled a lot?" he asked, hoping

phrasing it like a question would force her to give a little information about herself without him having to be too direct.

"Yup," she replied.

So much for that. "Business or pleasure?"

He heard her release a small sigh. She didn't reply right away, making him wonder if she was going to refuse to respond at all. Thankfully, after a few moments, she did. "I guess it was business. My parents have dragged me and my sister all over the place for as long as I can remember."

"What for?" His peripheral vision picked up her head turning toward him, so he quickly spared her a glance.

"That's number three," she said.

"Three what?"

"Your third question. You only get twenty, so make them count." She settled back in her seat. "My parents are greedy social climbers. They'd go to Mars if there was a payday at the end of it."

"What do they do for a living?"

"They're talent managers."

"What kind of talent do they look for?"

"Why? Got any hidden talents you want to pitch to them?"

Cole heard the smile in her words, which caused the corners of his own mouth to quirk up. "None that are legal to do in public."

Brooke laughed at that, which made warmth spread through Cole's chest. He liked making her laugh more than he'd ever admit out loud.

"They mostly represent children," she said, though her voice was so low when she said it he almost didn't hear her over the rumbling of Mary Sue.

Cole smiled. "They ever make you audition for anything? Please tell me there's some embarrassing commercial of you out there somewhere." He'd said it as a joke, but Brooke went silent on him again. He looked over at her and saw how tense she was. Just as he was about to tell her she didn't have to answer, she spoke again.

"I've always been a disappointment to them."

There was a sincerity in her voice that made the words ring true, but something about it made Cole feel...unsure. Like she was holding something back even though he didn't doubt she was being honest. He knew there was more to that story, but he also knew enough to know he'd taken the conversation as far as she wanted it to go. Probably even further, really, and he didn't want to push. "You and your sister close?" he asked, hoping that would direct them in a safer direction.

He noticed her relax a fraction as her eyes drifted back to the road ahead of them. "Yeah. Natasha's three years younger, but we've always been close. You have any siblings?"

"I had a brother. He died when we were kids."

Brooke spun toward him again. "I'm so sorry. I can't even imagine how devastating that would be."

"Yeah, we weren't super close. He was older than me by a couple of years, and I more annoyed him than anything else. But he looked out for me too. When he was gone, things were...worse. In every way." He didn't let himself think deeply about Brett often. It brought up a whole host of memories that were akin to a hornets' nest—impossible for him not to acknowledge. But he didn't want to go poking at it either. The loss of Brett had made an already fucked-up situation even more unbearable. He'd grown up most of his life with only their father, a man who had started out as mean as a rattlesnake and turned into a viper once Brett was gone, lashing out whenever the mood struck. Which was often.

"I'm...very sorry to hear that," Brooke said softly.

"It is what it is," Cole replied, because even though he hated that saying, there wasn't much else to say about it. "If you could be anything, what would it be?" He desperately wanted to get them off the subject of family. Even going there to begin with made him feel like a moron. He should've known it would come around to his own, and the only topic he wanted to get into less was his time overseas.

"A teacher," Brooke replied immediately.

"Really?" He was unable to keep the surprise out of his voice, which made Brooke glare at him.

"Yes, really."

The offended look on her face made Cole laugh, which only pissed her off more if her crossing her arms over her chest was any indication. "Sorry. I just didn't expect you to say that."

"Clearly," she grumbled.

"What would you teach?"

"I dunno. One of the arts maybe. Like music or drama or actual art. Even teaching dance would be fun."

"You can dance?"

"Yes."

"What kind?"

"Any kind. Well, that's not true. I can't ballroom dance. You're up to question number twelve by the way."

"No way. I haven't asked that many."

"Are you questioning my counting skills now?"

"Wouldn't dream of it, Princess." They were quiet for a couple of minutes. There was really only one more question Cole wanted the answer to, but he wasn't sure he should ask it. *He* wouldn't want to answer it if the roles were reversed, which they unavoidably would be. But he couldn't help himself. He had to know. "What are you running from, Brooke?"

She inhaled sharply and held it a second before letting it out slowly. He noticed her turn and look out the window. "Have you ever felt like your life was completely out of your control?"

"Yes," he answered honestly.

"I guess I just... There was no moving forward from where I was in my life. Any choice I made would have been the wrong one. So instead of making one, I took off."

"Wasn't taking off still making a choice?"

"I guess. But it was one *I* was in control of."

"Do you think it was the right or wrong choice?" Cole was almost afraid of this answer. Probably because the answer would reflect on him, and he didn't want to be responsible for anything that hurt Brooke.

She looked over at him, and he tore his gaze away from the road long enough to lock eyes with her. There was a smile on her lips, but it seemed a little sad. "I'm not sure yet. But I have a feeling it's going to end up being both."

It wasn't the reassuring answer Cole had been hoping for, but it was honest, and he couldn't ask more of her than that.

Cole wasn't sure what to say in response, so he took the

easy way out and brought things back to the game. "I feel like that last one should count for at least eight questions."

Brooke huffed out a laugh. "You won't get an argument from me."

"That's a first."

That caused her to snort. "Jerk," she murmured, though she managed to make the word sound affectionate.

"So I guess that makes it your turn."

"Nah," she said. "I'm going to save my questions for another time."

Relief and disappointment warred inside of him. While he was thankful for the reprieve, however temporary it may be, he was also more than a little sad Brooke didn't want to know more about him. Cole tried to shake the ridiculousness of that thought out of his head. This was a stranger he'd never see again after this trip. He reached over and cranked up the radio, ignoring the pang in his chest at the thought of becoming a distant memory for Brooke.

CHAPTER EIGHT

"Do you want me to drive? You know I have a license, and I don't mind taking a turn," Brooke said.

Cole briefly diverted his attention from the road to her. "We're a mile from Estes Park."

Her eyes narrowed slightly. "Should I know what that means?"

"It's the town that will take us onto Trail Ridge Road."

"Oh. Okay," Brooke said as she sat back in her seat. After a few moments of silence, she continued. "I'm assuming we've talked about what that road is."

Cole took a hand off the steering wheel and rubbed his forehead. "It helps to actually listen when people talk, Princess."

"I listen. Sometimes."

"Trail Ridge Road takes us across the Continental Divide. Do you remember talkin' about that?"

Brooke looked uncertain but nodded anyway. "It sounds vaguely familiar, but I don't know if that's because you said it or because I learned about it at some point."

"Okay, well, Trail Ridge is the highest paved road in the US and winds through the Rockies. The view's supposed to be amazin'."

"Awesome. I've never done anything touristy like this. I'm excited."

"What do you mean? I know you've taken vacations before," he said, chancing another quick look over at her, which allowed him to catch her rolling her eyes.

"Well, yeah, we've gone on vacations, but usually to beaches and resorts. I've never gone anywhere with the sole purpose to explore and take in the scenery."

"Hmm," Cole sounded in response.

"What does that mean?"

"What does what mean?" he asked.

"That noise you made."

Cole shrugged. "I was just thinking about how different our lives must have been growing up." And how different they probably still were. Cole didn't know much about Brooke's life, but it was clear that hers was very different from his.

"That's probably an understatement," she mumbled, but she didn't say it like she was thankful for it. It almost sounded like she thought *he* had the better childhood, and what a laughable thought that was. There wasn't a single person in his hometown who would've ever wanted to trade places with him, that was for sure.

"Estes Park is where I had you make us hotel reservations earlier. I figured we'd drive Trail Ridge, spend a few hours in Grand Lake on the other side, and then come back this way in case we missed anything along the highway the first time over it."

"That I remember doing."

"Good. Otherwise I'd have to have you analyzed for short-term memory loss."

"That diagnosis is still a distinct possibility."

Cole laughed in response. As he drove into the town, Cole was overwhelmed with how beautiful it was. With the Rockies providing a pristine backdrop, the town had a picturesque, idyllic quality that made Cole feel like he'd stepped into one of his childhood fantasies. He felt peaceful in a way he hadn't in a long time, if ever.

"This place is seriously awesome," Brooke said.

Cole turned to see her staring out of the passenger window, her nose practically pressed to the glass. The GPS on his phone guided them to their hotel. They checked in quickly before returning to the parking lot. Cole looked over at Brooke as he started his truck. "You want to start the trek over the Divide, or do you want to drive past the hotel that inspired *The Shining* first?"

Brooke's eyes widened. "*The Shining* as in *The* 'Redrum' *Shining*?"

The look of horror on her face made him laugh. "It's not where they filmed the movie. Stephen King stayed there, and it became his inspiration for the hotel in the movie."

"The Overlook Hotel."

"Guess you've seen the movie," Cole said with a teasing smirk.

"It was the first horror movie I ever saw. My sister and I sneaked downstairs one night after my parents went to sleep and found it on TV. I didn't sleep for months afterward. But in a bizarre way, I became fixated on it too. I'll watch it whenever it's on, even though it still scares the shit out of me."

"You are a highly complex person."

Brooke nodded sagely. "Totally."

"So is that a yes to going to see it or...?"

Brooke closed her eyes, and Cole saw a small shudder reverberate through her body. "Let's go later. I need to mentally prepare myself for it."

Cole chuckled as he put the car in gear and made his way toward Trail Ridge Road. The highway had multiple places to pull off the road so they could get out and take in the scenery. Cole took advantage of almost every opportunity to stop. He was so...amazed by it. As they stood side by side, overlooking a particularly serene view from a substantial elevation, Cole thought he'd found the definition of paradise. They'd both pulled hoodies out of their bags, though they still crossed their arms around themselves in an attempt to hold their warmth closer to their bodies.

"It makes you feel insignificant, doesn't it?" she asked suddenly.

Cole thought for a minute. He'd felt insignificant for most of his life, and he didn't think that description came anywhere close to describing how he felt in that moment. "I think I actually feel the opposite."

Her head jerked in his direction. "Really?"

"Yeah. Because I get to be here and see all of this. It makes me feel special. Lucky. Peaceful."

She looked at him for a few seconds, and then a few more, before turning back to the mountains surrounding them. "I guess I can see where you're coming from." Her tone was introspective, and maybe even a little bit sad, though Cole had no idea why that would be. He was on the verge of asking when she turned and began walking toward the car.

"I want to see this Continental Divide you've been going on about," she said over her shoulder as she rounded the car.

He stared after her for a second before following. Once he'd climbed in and started the engine, he said, "I don't think I've been 'going on' about it."

"You've probably said those two words more times in the past two hours than one of the local park rangers has in the past six months," Brooke teased. But the look on her face hinted she was enjoying Cole's excitement.

"That's ridiculous."

"And accurate."

"I'm having a good time. Can you not ruin it by picking a fight with me?" Cole said, his voice intentionally free of emotion.

"Are you implying that I ruin your good times? Because I seem to remember quite a few good times we've had over the past twenty-four hours that you seemed to enjoy immensely."

"Don't flirt with me either."

Brooke laughed. "You've got an awful lot of things I'm not allowed to do all of a sudden. Be careful, or I may have to start calling you Mom." Her voice started out light and playful, but the word "mom" came out of her mouth with a much harder edge to it.

"You flirtin' with me does *not* make me think motherly thoughts."

"Oh no? What do they make you think about?"

"Things that would get us arrested before we get to see

Milner's Pass."

"What's Milner's Pass?" she asked.

Jesus Christ, this girl was going to drive him nuts. "It's where the Continental Divide is. If I've been talkin' about it so much, how come you haven't picked up on that detail by now?"

"Because I've been blocking you out."

"Now that's not nice."

"I've been called a lot of things, cowboy. Nice has never been one of them."

He turned toward her briefly, just long enough for him to take in her wide smile and her bright eyes. She made a lot of comments like this—ones that hinted at how she'd been surrounded by people who may not have treated her with all that much respect or consideration. It angered him.

She broke his train of thought. "Don't look at me like that. You know firsthand that I'm an epic pain in the ass."

Yes, she could be. But that wasn't *all* she was. "I think you're nice and funny and honest and—"

"Now who's flirting with who?" she teased, though he saw it for the deflection it was. Brooke wasn't used to compliments. "For what it's worth, I think you're all those things too. And then some."

His smile grew, but he didn't reply, accepting the compliment as he wished she had done.

They arrived at their destination minutes later and got out of the car. It wasn't so much that it was the most beautiful spot on the highway, but it was damn cool. They were over ten thousand feet up and were in the exact spot that filtered water toward one ocean or the other. It didn't get much cooler than that.

There was a trail that some people were navigating, but Brooke and Cole had both agreed they didn't need to stray too far from the car. Neither one of them had appropriate clothes for hiking, and Cole didn't like undertaking adventures he wasn't prepared for.

"Have you ever had sex outside?" Brooke asked out of nowhere.

The question shocked him so thoroughly he felt his mouth open and close a few times as he processed what she'd said. "What?" was his eloquent response.

"Have. You. Ever. Had. Sex. Outside?"

"Yes. I. Have," he replied, mimicking her tone.

"I haven't."

"I haven't since I was a teenager, but it happened a few times back then."

She twisted her lips as though she was thinking hard about something, before she went back to the truck, fished around in one of her bags for a minute, and then started off down a trail.

It took Cole a second to respond before he jogged after her. "Where are you going?"

"To have sex in the woods."

"By yourself?" he asked with jest in his tone.

"Am I by myself right now?"

"You didn't exactly invite me along."

She looked him up and down. "Doesn't seem like you needed an invitation. Though if you're not interested, I'm sure I could proposition a random hiker."

A growl escaped him at her words—a sound Cole would deny until his dying day. "Like hell you will."

♦ ♦ ♦ ♦

Brooke wasn't sure what had come over her, but she liked it. Her tight jeans rubbed against her sensitive clit with every step, making it clear how on board her body was with the plan.

While Brooke had been in previous relationships, most of them had lacked passion. It had been two superficial people partaking in superficial things. But everything with Cole felt real in a way that made Brooke want more. More spontaneity, more adventure, more behavior that would give her parents an aneurysm if they ever heard about them. *This* was how life was supposed to be. And she was suddenly overwhelmed with the desire to live every fucking millisecond of it.

She walked down the trail a ways before veering off. It was chilly up here—bordering on downright cold. But the heat in her veins spurred her on as she made her way into the tree line with confidence.

"I'm not sure I want you in charge of leadin' us somewhere," Cole quipped from behind her.

"What if I told you you're going to really like where we're heading?" she replied, a smirk appearing on her lips even though he couldn't see her.

"I wouldn't be followin' you if I wasn't sure of that. It's what happens later, when we're lost and getting mauled by a grizzly, that I'm less thrilled about."

Brooke stopped dead in her tracks. "Wait? Are there bears here?"

"It's a giant wilderness. There's probably all sorts of predators out here."

Turning, Brooke stared at him. "Way to kill the mood."

Cole looked down to where the hard ridge of his cock was outlined in his pants. "I haven't killed my mood," he said, a laugh following the words out of his mouth.

There was nothing unappealing about the man. His Levi's, which were normally a little loose when his cock wasn't taking up all the available space, the dark-blue hoodie that made his blond hair look even lighter, the confident stance of a soldier who knew he could handle himself. Even the talk of killer bears fled to the recesses of her mind as she stepped closer to him. "Mine neither."

She wasn't sure who initiated the kiss. They both seemed to move toward each other as if they were each other's gravity, keeping them both tethered to adjoining orbits of passion. The kiss wasn't fast or slow, hard or soft. It was a fusion of lips that ignited a fire inside of Brooke.

In a sort of unspoken agreement, they didn't dawdle. Knowing someone could stumble upon them at any moment was part of the thrill, but it was also not an incident they actually wanted to have happen. The excitement was in the possibility, not in the actualization.

Cole thumbed open the button of her jeans and pulled the zipper down. She did the same, pushing them low enough that his thick cock could pop free. Then she slid her hand into the front pocket of her sweatshirt, withdrew the condom she'd retrieved from the car, and handed it to Cole.

He took it from her and tore it open, and as he sheathed himself, she wiggled her jeans down before turning around, bracing herself against a tree, and sticking her ass back toward him, presenting herself to him. It was the most exposed and vulnerable she'd ever been on purpose, and it was more empowering than she ever would have thought.

Stepping toward her, Cole ran a hand over her ass and let it trail between her legs. "You standin' here like this might just be the hottest thing I've ever seen."

"I'm going to need you to do more than see it." She rocked back so her ass brushed against his cock, causing Cole's hand to clamp down on her hip.

He rubbed his cock between her ass cheeks a few times before lining himself up and pushing inside of her. A groan left him that made him sound primal, like he belonged in the forest with the wild animals.

Brooke loved that she brought that out in him. She used her hands on the tree to push herself back onto him as he thrust forward. The slapping of skin between them was loud and not as inconspicuous as they probably should have been, but who the hell cared about being quiet when she was being fucked like she was being claimed?

There wasn't much buildup toward orgasm. She'd been turned on from the start, making the end point within reach as soon as he'd slid inside of her. If his harsh pants were any indication, Cole was right there with her.

His cock rubbed over the sensitive spot inside of her over and over again, lighting her up until spark met fuse, and she combusted around him with a loud moan. Her legs shook with the sensation as he continued to drive into her, his motions becoming more erratic the closer he got to his own orgasm.

His hips seemed to stutter seconds later before he pushed

deep one final time, letting his chest blanket over her as his forehead pressed into one of her shoulder blades. His body shivered as he emptied into the condom, his chest heaving against her back as he tried to catch his breath.

They were both still for a few moments, enjoying the afterglow and letting the intensity drain from their bodies before they attempted to move. Eventually they had to move, however. Cole tied up the condom and wrapped it in some leaves before sliding it into the front pouch of his hoodie. They both righted their clothes and started the trek back toward the trail without a word between them. They'd said everything they needed to with their bodies.

◆ ◆ ◆ ◆

They stopped a few more times on the way across Trail Ridge Road before arriving in the town of Grand Lake on the other side. It was beautiful there, and they wandered around for about an hour before they figured it best to get back to Estes Park before dark. After stopping a few times on the return trip to see some scenery they hadn't gotten enough of on the way over the first time, they returned to their hotel with a couple hours of daylight left.

After they'd both showered and gotten dressed, Cole asked, "Do you want to grab something quick to eat before heading over to the Stanley Hotel?"

Brooke sighed. "You're determined to give me nightmares, aren't you?"

Cole laughed at her dramatics. "You said you'd go."

"I say lots of things I don't mean. Like when I said I liked you."

Cole shook his head, a smile etched on his face. "I don't exactly remember you ever sayin' that, Princess."

"Oh. Well, good." She turned away from him to pack some clothes back into her bag, and Cole couldn't resist, walking up behind her and wrapping his arms around her.

The move felt both odd and natural to him. As if he'd been doing it his whole life but in an alternate universe. "Come on, Princess. All work and no play makes Cole a dull boy."

She turned around and smacked him, which caused him to laugh loudly. He leaned down and pressed a soft kiss to her neck. He felt her melt into him, letting her arms wrap around his shoulder. They stood there like that for a couple of minutes, and Cole was struck by how content he was to simply hug—and be hugged by—her.

Finally, she let out a deep breath and said, "Okay. I'm ready."

They pulled away from each other, but Cole instantly missed the contact. He laced his fingers with hers and pulled her toward the door. "We'll have fun. I promise."

She didn't reply but squeezed his hand, which he took as a sign of agreement. They went to a small café across the street from their hotel for dinner before climbing into Cole's truck and heading for the famous hotel.

He figured he'd drive around the premises of the hotel first before they got out and explored on foot. He was taking everything in when he heard Brooke gasp beside him.

"No fucking way," she whispered.

"What?" he asked, his head swiveling around to see what she could mean.

"They have a fucking maze here. I hate mazes."

"Who hates mazes?" Cole took in the distaste on her face. Even grimacing, she looked adorable.

"Someone who was once lost in a haunted corn maze for three hours when she was twelve. Then add in the fact that *The Shining* is one of the scariest movies of all time..."

"I don't know if I'd say scariest of all time."

"You didn't. I did." She shook her head. "I'm serious. I'm not going in there, so don't even ask."

"I'm not askin'," he replied. "I'm tellin' you. We are absolutely going in there."

Crossing her arms over her chest, she sank back into her seat. "I'm not."

He laughed. "We'll just have to see, won't we?"

"You make it sound as if you can out-stubborn me. You can't, and you won't."

Cole pulled the truck into a parking spot and cut the ignition. "Whatever you say."

In her defense, it took him over an hour to get her into the maze. They'd walked the perimeter of the hotel twice and went in to see the lobby before he managed to lead her in the right direction without her realizing it. Once they were at the entrance to the "hedged hell," as Brooke called it, it took some serious convincing to get her inside.

"I didn't realize you were such a wimp. This tough-girl act you got goin' on is just that, huh? An act."

"I stopped giving in to peer pressure in middle school,"

she retorted.

"I'm not pressuring. Just stating facts."

"Your facts are meaningless to me. You want to go die in a sculpted torture chamber, be my guest. I'll stay out here and maybe even call for help when I hear you getting murdered with an ax."

Cole looked up at the sky. "It's gettin' dark. If we don't go in soon, it'll *really* be dangerous."

"Not dangerous for me, since I don't plan on going in at all."

"We're goin' in, Princess."

"*We* are doing no such thing."

Cole sighed. "Have it your way." With that, he dipped down, grabbed her by the back of the thighs, and hoisted her over his shoulder. He sped inside the maze before her squalling could attract a crowd.

"Cole, you better put me down, or I swear to God, I'll redrum you."

He laughed, taking her deeper into the maze before setting her down. "Okay, we're in. Now to find our way out."

She looked around, clearly confused about which way they'd even come from since she'd been upside down. "I'm seriously so pissed at you right now."

"You gotta face your fears," he said. "It'll be fun. I promise."

She reached out and gripped his hand tightly. "You better get me out of here in one piece."

He gave her hand a squeeze. "Always."

It took two dead-ends and a shortcut through a hedge to get them both laughing like high school kids.

"I can't believe how complicated this is," she said. "Can't you use your army skills and get us out of here?"

"Sorry. I must've missed the maze course during basic training."

"Too busy learning all the ninja moves you used in that bar?"

Cole's head whirled toward her, but she kept staring straight ahead. It was the first time she'd brought up the bar since it had all gone down. He hoped that her referencing it so casually meant she'd found a way to move beyond it. Knowing a thing or two about feeling powerless in a situation, Cole had hoped the event didn't cause too much trauma. There was no forgetting it—Cole knew that—but she seemed to be dealing with it well, and for that Cole was thankful. "Among other things," he replied, and she didn't ask him any more about it.

It was dusk by the time they reached the exit, which they only found because Cole had put Brooke on his shoulders so she could see which way to go. Truthfully, Cole felt like he could've had them out of the maze much more quickly, but he'd been having too much fun being "lost" with Brooke, so he'd let her lead the way.

Afterward, they got back in the truck and drove around Estes Park until they saw an ice cream shop and decided to stop. Cole paid for their cones and then ushered Brooke to a small table. The shop was in a busy part of town, and it seemed like everyone had the same idea they had. The place was mobbed.

They were talking about their favorite parts of the day when Brooke stopped responding. He looked over at her and immediately felt himself tense at how pale she looked. "What's wrong?" he asked.

She didn't seem to hear him as she stared toward the front of the shop.

He tried to follow her gaze, but there were too many people to be able to tell who she was looking at. "Brooke?"

She started and stood abruptly. "We gotta go."

"What? Why?" He stood with her and followed her to the trash can, where she threw away her cone before starting toward the car.

He fell into step with her and tried asking her again what was wrong.

"Nothing," she answered. "Just don't feel very well all of the sudden."

He tried talking to her a few more times as they drove back to the hotel, but all she'd say was that she wasn't feeling well. He could tell she was getting annoyed with him, so he decided to leave it alone for a bit. But one thing was sure: he'd need to get to the bottom of her freak-out before they went any farther.

CHAPTER NINE

Cole spent the rest of the night wondering what the best plan of action was. He didn't want to force Brooke to discuss something she clearly had no interest in talking about. At least not with him. And he couldn't blame her. As far as she was concerned, Cole was just some country boy who'd offered her a ride somewhere. Or nowhere. She knew basically nothing about him other than his name and address, and he didn't know much more about her. Though he wanted to know what her deal was, there was no reason she should have to tell him her most personal secrets, and Cole understood that.

Except the more he thought about it, the more he'd convinced himself that she *should* have to tell him about all of her shit. Or at least *some* of it. Because as much as whatever she was running from was her business, at a certain point, it became his business too. And that point was when she'd forced him to leave the place abruptly and with absolutely no explanation. Cole had no issue protecting her; he'd done it once before, and he'd sure as shit do it again if he had to. But since Brooke had refused to tell him who the enemy was, he decided he'd have to find out for himself.

He knew there was no guarantee that googling Brooke would provide him with any information he didn't already know. It would probably only result in some dated Facebook account or information about her college volleyball team or something. It wasn't like he suspected she had a warrant out for her arrest in some other state that would come up with a few clicks on the internet. But he knew there was a chance *something* might result from a search. And *something* was better than nothing.

He waited until Brooke went into the bathroom and he heard the shower turn on before taking out his phone. On the off chance the search resulted in something disturbing, he didn't want her there for his reaction. He walked toward the window to get a better signal before opening up Google and typing in "Brooke Alba." Hitting the search button, he prepared himself one more time for all of the fucked-up scenarios he could imagine. Maybe she was wanted for grand theft auto or for knocking over a liquor store or for squishing a fucking praying mantis with a designer heel.

The possibilities were endless, and each one caused his pulse to speed up. Especially the ones that involved Brooke running from something that someone did *to* her rather than something she did herself. He tried not to focus on how messed up it was that he'd rather read about her skipping bail on a drug trafficking charge than see her name come up on some sort of restraining order she'd put on an abusive ex.

But no matter how many ideas popped into Cole's head before his search, none of them were close to the reality.

♦ ♦ ♦

Shutting off the shower, Brooke ran a towel through her short hair. She wasn't sure that she'd ever get used to how quickly it dried or how little time it took to style it. Every time she looked in the mirror, there was still an element of shock when she saw her reflection. It wasn't like she *expected* to see her long dark hair. Logically she knew she wouldn't. It was more like the air where it used to be still held a place for her hair's memory, like some kind of supernatural ghost limb.

She put some lotion on her body and pulled on some cotton shorts and a soft T-shirt, which she figured wouldn't stay on long anyway once she climbed into bed with Cole. But before she could think any more about the two of them naked and rolling around in bed together, a sound from outside the door made her freeze. She wasn't sure she was actually hearing what she thought she was hearing since the music had been so low at first. But gradually, as the song continued, there was no denying what it was. And though she hoped it was only a coincidence that Cole was playing the single from her first album, she wasn't naïve enough to actually believe that it was. The ex-military Southern charmer wasn't exactly a huge fan of teen pop.

She'd had her hand on the doorknob for at least thirty seconds as she decided how to address the situation before Cole's voice interrupted her internal dialogue. "Come on out, Brooke. Come dance with me." He didn't say anything else directly to her, but she could hear him trying to sing along with a song he clearly hadn't heard until now.

"What the hell are you doing?" she asked after pulling open the door and heading out into the hotel room.

"What does it look like?" he asked. "Dancing."

Brooke thought about telling him the weird jumping and head-bobbing he was doing only counted as dancing if you were in preschool, but she had an agenda she needed to pursue. And that involved finding out exactly what Cole knew about her.

"I love this song," he said. "Don't you?"

"Turn it off," she practically yelled over the music.

He continued his awkward jerks like she hadn't even spoken.

"Cole!"

His eyes had been shut as he pretended to be caught up in the beat, but when she screamed his name, they shot open. "What?" he yelled back before finally bringing the volume down to a level where she could barely hear it.

"You think this is funny?" she asked. Her arms were crossed, and her jaw went rigid after her question. She regretted ever telling Cole her last name. At the time, she'd figured keeping her stage name to herself would be enough to conceal her identity. Clearly that wasn't the case.

The corner of Cole's lips lifted into a goofy smile, but for the first time, it was anything but cute. "Kinda," he said. "When were you gonna tell me you're famous?"

"I wasn't. And I'm not *famous*." That description, oddly enough, was exactly what she'd been trying to avoid when she'd decided to get the hell out of Philly.

Cole raised an eyebrow at her. "You're pretty famous," he said simply.

"I can't be *that* famous. You didn't know who I was until about five minutes ago. How did you find out anyway? Google me?"

"Yeah." He paused for a moment to turn her song off when it started over again. "Wait. Why do you seem mad?"

"Because I am. That was a complete invasion of privacy." Even as the words left her lips, she knew how ridiculous the accusation was.

"It wasn't an invasion of privacy. It was an internet search. And a pretty easy one. I typed in your name, and I clicked on the first link that popped up." He seemed to be assessing her mood as he spoke, and she tried to make it clear that his explanation did nothing to lessen her anger. "Are you seriously bothered by this? You're in the public eye all the time, from what I can tell. What's one more person?"

She hated how casual his explanation sounded, like he couldn't give a fuck less that she was irritated. "Don't even act like I'm a psycho. If I wanted you to know I was some pop star who middle school girls sing to at sleepovers, I would've told you." This was exactly the kind of shit that made her want to get away in the first place—people wanting to know her business, looking into every detail of her existence. Sure, not everyone knew who she was. And she was certainly thankful for that. But she wouldn't have any fucking chance of living a normal life if she kept on the path she was headed.

Cole tossed his phone onto the bed with more force than was necessary and stretched his jaw as he ran a hand over his stubble. He looked as irritated as she was, though she didn't know how that was possible. "Listen, Princess. I'm gonna be honest here. You're gonna have to get over yourself, because I don't give two shits who you are or how much money you have. I don't care how many little girls dress up as you for Halloween or download your songs to the phones that their mommies and daddies pay for. None of that shit matters to me. You want to know what I do care about?" He didn't wait for her to answer before he continued. "Us. And our fucking safety. I asked you why the hell you wanted to leave suddenly today, and you wouldn't tell me. For all I knew, there was some abusive ex-fucking-boyfriend there trying to hunt you down, so I googled you to try to find out who was chasin' us. That's it. Stop acting like I went through your fucking trash or something."

"Stop cursing. And stop calling me Princess."

"Then stop being so secretive," he snapped back. "If someone's after you, they're after *us*. I have a right to know that."

"No one's after me. Not yet at least. And for the record"—her voice was louder now—"I'd have hoped you'd know me better by now than to think I'd put you in some kind of danger."

"The bar in Kansas wasn't dangerous?"

This motherfucker couldn't be serious. "Don't you dare blame me for that," she warned.

Cole rubbed his neck with his hand. "You're right. That was uncalled for. But come on, Brooke. You act like I violated your privacy or something. You're famous. Doesn't having your business available at the click of a button kind of come with the territory?"

Brooke took a deep breath in an attempt to sound calm, even though she was anything but. "I got my first contract when I was fourteen. I was too young to understand what I was getting myself into, and I sure as hell wasn't prepared for life in the spotlight. People critiquing my every move, every hairstyle, every outfit. You think judgment's bad in high school? Try living life in the public eye. I had no idea what all of it was gonna be like." She hadn't meant to let all of that out so quickly—or at all—but it was the truth. And Cole needed to hear it. She shook her head, her anger dissipating as sadness began to replace it. "Just when I was actually enjoying being with someone who knew me as Brooke Alba and not Brooke Devereaux, you had to go and ruin that," she said. Then she snatched her bag off the dresser and headed for the door. But before she opened it, she turned back to look at him. She thought she saw a hint of remorse on his face, but it was too late to make her feel any better. She did allow her voice to soften a bit though as she said one last thing before leaving. "For once it was nice not to be somebody."

CHAPTER TEN

Brooke knew that running off again was stupid. God only knew what would've happened to her last time if Cole hadn't shown up. She didn't even want to think about it, but the memory had imprinted on her deeply enough to keep her from leaving the hotel. She found an empty banquet hall that was dimly lit and went inside. There weren't any chairs out, so she leaned against a wall and sank to the floor.

If she let herself be rational, she couldn't blame Cole for what he'd done. But he'd fucked everything up. She'd had such a good time being herself—such fun learning who the hell she even was—and now it was done. Because she wouldn't be Brooke Alba, the hitchhiking pain in his ass anymore. She'd be Brooke Devereaux, the B-list pop singer who'd been portrayed in the media as a vapid fame whore for the past ten years. Would he even want to call her Princess anymore now that he probably thought she was some rich spoiled brat?

Tears stung her eyes, and she swiped at them angrily. Why did everything always get so fucked up? For all she knew, Cole was upstairs at that very second calling some tabloid to sell his story. Though as quickly as she thought it, she dismissed it. Brooke wasn't certain about much, but she did know Cole would never betray her like that.

Though she also knew things would be different from here on out. Even if he let her still travel with him, he'd treat her differently. Brooke cursed the moment they decided to stop for ice cream. She'd seen all the teenage girls there with their families, but she'd had such a great day—such a normal, great day—that she'd forgotten for a while she was mildly famous. But when she'd seen the group of three girls whispering and pointing in her direction, the truth had slammed back into her, and all she could think about was getting the hell out of there.

If she hadn't acted like such a crazy person, maybe Cole wouldn't have noticed anything was even up with her. But no, she'd practically sprinted to the truck, barely talked to him on the drive back to the hotel, and then locked herself in the bathroom.

Brooke bumped her head back against the wall as she realized those girls could have already splashed it all over social media that they'd seen her. And while a sighting of her wasn't actually big news, it might get noticed by someone who was looking. Namely her parents.

She pulled her phone out of her pocket, thankful she'd grabbed it on her way out of the room, and called her sister.

"Hey, Brooke. I'm so glad you called." Natasha's voice sounded rushed, and it immediately made Brooke tense.

"Why? What's wrong?"

Natasha sighed. "I think it's time to come home, Brooke."

"What? Why?"

"Mom and Dad are seriously freaking out. They're talking about getting the authorities involved. Saying you've been missing and possibly kidnapped. Shit is getting fucking intense around here."

"They wouldn't. There's no way they could keep that under wraps." But even as Brooke said the words, she knew they were hollow.

Which was only confirmed when Natasha gave a humorless laugh. "How quickly you forget. Any publicity is good publicity to them. They won't care if it gets out as long as it also gets you back home."

"Why is everything always such a clusterfuck?" Brooke muttered.

"Listen, I get it. I really do. I can't even imagine the pressure they put you under. But...isn't enough enough? I mean, running away isn't the most mature thing in the world."

"I'm *not* running away. I'm a fucking adult, and if I want to go across the country or across the fucking world, then that's my right."

Natasha was quiet for a minute and then said, "You're right. It is. But it's not like you just took a trip out of the blue. You *are* running, Brooke. All because you can't just say no to them."

Brooke stood, her anger causing her to pace. "Because you're so great at telling them no? How's that business degree treating you?" It was a low blow. Brooke knew that, but she didn't care. If Natasha was going to call her out on kowtowing to their parents, then Brooke wasn't above reminding her that she was getting forced into a career she had no interest in at all because their parents wanted Natasha to be able to manage Brooke's money.

"At least I didn't take off on a Greyhound."

"Because you don't have the balls to."

"Yeah, it takes a lot of courage to be a twenty-four-year-old runaway."

"Screw you, Natasha. I really don't need this shit right now."

"And I do? I feel like I'm living with the KGB right now. They're constantly making calls, logging potential sightings. The den looks like a goddamn war room."

Brooke was silent for a few seconds, and when she spoke next, she couldn't keep her voice from breaking. "I didn't ask for any of this."

Natasha sighed. "I know. But I didn't either. And they're getting crazy. You know how they can be."

"I can't come home. The deadline's almost here. I just need to last two more weeks."

"Maybe just call them, then. Because even though they care about the deal, they're also worried about you. They're still your parents."

Brooke wasn't sure how true that was. They'd been more managers than parents for so long, Brooke no longer knew which of their emotions were familial and which were professional. But maybe Natasha was right. If they really were genuinely concerned for her safety, maybe hearing from her would go a long way to make them stop forcing her into things she had no interest in. "Okay. I'll give them a call."

Natasha breathed a sigh of what Brooke guessed was relief. "Good. I'm not saying you have to tell them where you are. But I bet just hearing from you will keep them from doing anything over the top."

"I hope so."

Natasha was quiet again for a few moments before she said, "I love you, Brooke. I'm sorry if I was a bitch."

"Me too. I love you too." And Brooke did. Her sister was the only one who knew just how complicated her life had been. But while she knew it, she didn't always *understand* it. She didn't know what it was like to actually have to live with someone else calling all of the shots and leaving you no choice but to live out the consequences of those shots in the public eye. Sure, their parents had picked Natasha's college major, but they'd picked Brooke's last two boyfriends, her friend-group, as well as most of her wardrobe. Brooke hadn't been in any semblance of control over her life until she'd gotten into a truck with a cowboy just under a week ago.

Had it really only been a few days? Brooke felt like she'd squeezed more living into the past week than she had into the twenty-four preceding years. And it wasn't something she was willing to give up. Not now. Probably not ever.

But the first step in keeping things on her terms was to stay away just a little bit longer. Her parents always had a way of manipulating her into bending to their wills. But they couldn't control what was beyond their grasp.

Brooke and Natasha said their goodbyes, and Brooke stared at her phone, knowing what she needed to do but not wanting any part of actually doing it.

◆ ◆ ◆ ◆

Cole fought with himself for fifteen minutes before his concern overrode his anger and he went to look for Brooke. He knew she was a grown woman and had a right to her space, but he also couldn't forget the last time she'd gone off half-cocked. If anything happened to her, Cole would never forgive himself.

Hoping she'd remained in the hotel, Cole searched all over. He was just about to head back up to the room to see if she'd returned, when he saw a hallway off the main lobby. A quick look around showed that no one was paying him any mind, so he set off down the hall, which had a door at the end. It made him think of the scene in *The Shining*, where the little boy saw the creepy twins, but Cole shook off the thought. It wasn't the time to be dramatic.

He opened the door a crack and peeped inside. It was so dim he had to step inside in order to see. He let his eyes rove over the space, almost missing the small figure sitting against a wall at first glance. A sigh of relief left him as he thrust his hands into his pockets. Now that he knew she was safe, part of him wondered if he should head back upstairs and leave her be. But the way she was curled in on herself, hugging her knees, made him want to comfort her, despite the agitation still riding him.

Approaching slowly, Cole cleared his throat so he wouldn't startle her. She didn't move an inch. He sat down beside her, letting his arms rest on his bent knees, and waited. And waited.

Finally, after a few minutes of silence, she spoke. "I'm sorry for taking off."

The words were said in such a toneless way, it immediately washed away the majority of Cole's irritation. He didn't want to fight with Brooke. His buddies in the army had always ribbed him about him having a hero complex, and he realized how true it was in that moment. Cole wanted to be the guy who protected her and put a smile on her face, and the strength of that desire kind of scared him a little. "No worries. I'm just glad you're okay."

She let out a snort. "I wouldn't quite go that far. I don't think I've been okay for a very long time."

She twirled her phone in her hand, and Cole wondered who she'd talked to and what had been said. But the coldness of her words struck him a little dumb. He must have hesitated too long because she looked over at him and apologized.

"I shouldn't have said that. I don't want to make my problems your problems."

"Just spill it, Princess," he said, hoping she heard the teasing in his voice.

She huffed a laugh, which made a sense of relief spread through him. Letting her head thud back against the wall, she stared up at the ceiling. "I'm a little...lost."

"Well, with your navigational skills, that's not all that surprising."

Her laugh was fuller this time. "Ass." She straightened her legs and let her phone rest on one of her thighs. "Have you ever felt like you've made so many mistakes that you're no longer capable of doing anything right?"

God, did Cole know how that felt. There were so many things that plagued Cole's mind, he wondered how he ever thought of anything else. But this wasn't about him. He didn't want to get into all the ways he felt he'd failed over the years. Maybe later, but not now. So he simply said, "Of course."

"The singing... I never wanted any of that. Don't get me

wrong, it was cool for a while, but I'm not really built for it, ya know? You call me Princess, and I know that name fits in some ways, but the truth is I don't like a lot of attention. I hate having to worry that people will recognize me while I'm out, or that one day I'll be even *more* famous and I won't even be able to go out and do normal things."

"Like see the Rocky Mountains?" Cole asked.

Her head slanted to one side so she could look at him. "Exactly like that." She smiled, but it had a sad quality to it that made his heart hurt.

"If it's not what you want, why do you do it?"

She shifted again so she was no longer looking at him. "That's the million-dollar question. I know I'm an adult, so saying I don't have a choice is stupid, but it feels that way. My parents have run my career since before I was old enough to realize that they don't particularly care what I want. And by the time I was old enough to see it, it was...too late. I'd committed to things I couldn't have gotten out of even if I'd been brave enough to try."

"That makes sense for the past, but what about the future? Going forward, you can make the decisions."

When she didn't reply right away, he looked over at her and saw a tear slide down her cheek. He wanted to wrap his arm around her but didn't feel like that was what *she* would want. And in light of what they were discussing, he knew it was important for this to go in whatever direction she wanted it to.

"When you've given up control for your entire life, it can be really hard to get it back. Even thinking about it is overwhelming."

"Hard doesn't mean impossible," he said softly.

"No. Not impossible," she said on a breath. She didn't sound so sure, but Cole didn't call her on her obvious self-doubt.

"Are they who you were talking to?" he asked as he nodded his head toward her phone.

Brooke looked down at it as if she'd forgotten it was there. "No, my sister. She thinks I need to come home and face the music, so to speak. But...I need more time. I know running isn't the answer, but until I have a better one, it's what I'm going to stick with. I only need a couple more weeks."

"What happens in a couple more weeks?"

Brooke started picking at the polish on her fingernail. "There's a tour I was invited to open for. We're supposed to announce the news and sign the contracts in two weeks. But"—she looked over at him—"I can't sign it if I'm not there."

Cole let out a breath. "I'm not tryin' to sound like a dick here, but you are an adult, Brooke. You can just refuse to sign it."

Brooke shrugged. "I can. But I won't. My parents have an uncanny way of getting in my head. Always have. I can't trust myself not to cave. The only way to keep them out of here," she said as she tapped her temple with her finger, "is to keep them away from me entirely."

They were both quiet for a minute. Cole was letting her words sink in. It wasn't that he couldn't relate to how deeply a parent could fuck up their child. Parental mind games weren't foreign to him. It was harder to understand a grown adult running away instead of facing the problem head-on, but the more he thought about it, the more he realized his own actions could be interpreted in a similar way. And who the hell was he to judge anyway? No one was going to give him any awards for emotional maturity. "You wanna go back upstairs? My ass is falling asleep."

Brooke looked at him like he was insane for a second before snorting out a laugh. "Yeah, mine too."

He stood and then pulled Brooke to her feet. He kept hold of her hand all the way back to their room. They got ready for bed in silence, but when he slid into bed beside her, she turned toward him and laid her head on his chest. Wrapping his arm around her tightly, Cole gave her a soft kiss on the top of her head. "So I guess this means I'm stuck with you for at least two more weeks, huh?"

"Yup. At least." She snuggled closer to him as if she were trying to burrow into his skin.

And damn if he didn't like both her words and the feel of her beside him. But he couldn't bring himself to cop to either thing out loud. Instead, he murmured "Okay" and hoped the way he held her was enough to say what his words didn't.

CHAPTER ELEVEN

"Are we there yet?" Brooke had asked that same question at least five times in the last hour or so, mainly because she enjoyed seeing Cole roll his eyes or shake his head at her as he turned up the radio.

"You know how you'll know when we're there?" he asked over the Luke Bryan song.

It occurred to her that weeks ago she wouldn't have known who sang this. And she definitely wouldn't have enjoyed it. But somehow she was starting to like Cole's choice in music almost as much as she was starting to like him. "How?" she asked back.

"We'll actually *be* there. Unless you see a sign that says Arches National Park, we're not there yet.

"Smartass," she said with a laugh. "I thought you were gonna be serious."

"I was. Actually," he said, handing her his phone. "Can you look to see what the webcam looks like? We're only about ten minutes away."

"Webcam?" What the hell was he talking about? She took the phone from him as she waited for him to reply.

"The park has a webcam near the gate because it gets backed up sometimes. There's an entrance road right off one ninety-one, and you're not allowed to stop on the highway to wait to get into the park."

"So do we just loop around or something until it clears?"

"Not sure if that's easy to do or not. But check the webcam before you start panickin'."

A few moments later, Brooke was on the park's website scrolling through all of the tips and pictures. It looked absolutely beautiful, with natural stone arches of various textures and colors, beautiful sunsets. "It says the best time to go is the early morning or evening and that summer gets the most crowded. Did you see that when you looked on the site?"

"Yeah," he answered casually.

"Then why are we here in the middle of the afternoon in August?"

Cole laughed. "Well, I don't control the seasons, Princess. And I didn't wanna leave any later this morning because if we hit too much traffic, it might be too dark to go at all."

She didn't reply but continued to scroll for more information. "It says if the entrance road's too crowded that it's best to come back another time."

"Check the webcam, Brooke," Cole said again. "I'm sure it'll be fine."

"Says the person who brought us here during the absolute busiest time possible," she said, causing Cole to laugh again. She was beginning to wonder if he did this shit for the sole purpose of driving her nuts, but she decided not to ask. The webcam took a while to load, but when it finally did, she turned the phone to face him. "Look. You see all those cars?"

Cole shot a glance in her direction. "Oh shit. It's totally backed up," he said, sounding way more shocked than he should've been. Then he shrugged. "We still gotta find someplace to stay anyway. Why don't we come back in the morning or somethin'? We aren't in any rush. And it'll be better after a good night's sleep. I'm beat anyway."

"Your optimism should be way more impressive than it is," she said dryly.

"Why thank you," he said with a smile that couldn't help but put one on her own face too.

Leaning against the seat, she rolled her head toward Cole. "Okay, tomorrow it is, then. She'd already grabbed Cole's phone again and was using the GPS to find nearby hotels. She clicked on the one that had four stars and was only seven minutes away and hit Go. "Well, now I'll need to figure out something to keep me occupied, since you're exhausted and probably want to go right to sleep."

"Whoa there a second. I didn't say I was going to go right to sleep."

The hand he put on her thigh had her hoping they found a hotel soon so she didn't have to add the shoulder of a highway to her list of places she'd had sex in public. "Screw Arches Park," she said. "Tell Mary Sue to speed it up."

Cole barked out a laugh. "Trust me, if I could get Mary Sue to go any faster, I would." He patted the dashboard gingerly, and it seemed to shake even more than it was already rattling from the high speed.

"She won't go any faster?" Brooke asked. "All this time I thought you were just being cautious. I didn't realize"—she leaned over to look at the speedometer—"that Mary's max speed was sixty-seven. How old is this thing anyway? You never told me."

"A lady never reveals her age."

"Untrue. I'm twenty-four."

"My statement stands," Cole joked, and Brooke gave him a hard swat to his bicep.

"I'm a lady," she said.

"You peed on the side of the road like fifteen miles back."

Brooke laughed loudly, shifting in her seat so she could face him better. "Don't pretend like you didn't do that too."

Cole shrugged. "I'm not. But I'm not the one claimin' to be a lady."

"That's totally unfair. It's a double-standard. Just because I don't have a dick doesn't mean I can't go to the bathroom outside. What were we even talking about?" Brooke asked, wanting to steer the conversation in a different direction.

"Mary Sue."

"Right. So you're really not going to tell me how old your car is?"

"First of all, she's not a car. She's a truck. And second, she's sensitive about her age. I don't wanna embarrass her."

"You realize she's not alive, right? Because I thought you were kidding at first, but now I'm not so sure."

Cole rubbed a hand over the worn leather of the steering wheel and let out a soft laugh. Letting an arm hang out of the window, he opened his hand so the air pressed against it as he drove. Suddenly he seemed to be somewhere else, like the road ahead of him might allow him to escape whatever he was thinking about.

"You okay?" she asked, mainly because she knew he

wasn't but didn't want to ask a more specific question if he wasn't ready to answer it.

Brooke watched Cole smooth his tongue over his teeth pensively. "She's twenty-five," he said, not letting his gaze leave the highway.

Something told her that if she remained silent, he'd fill it with whatever was on his mind, so she stayed quiet. Her eyes were on the road too, but she let them drift to Cole as he drove for another minute or so without speaking.

"My brother got her a few months before he passed." That was all he said at first, but soon enough he spoke again. "Took him over a year of cuttin' grass and baggin' groceries before he had enough money to buy her. And then she didn't even run. Least for a bit 'til he fixed her up."

She remembered Cole mentioning his brother's death, but all he'd said about it was that things had gotten worse after it.

"Brett didn't even get a chance to really drive her before he died. Just up the street a few times even though my dad woulda lost it if he knew. Brett didn't even have a permit, let alone a license. He died two weeks before he turned sixteen."

Brooke hadn't asked any questions when Cole had brought up his brother the first time, but now she found herself desperately wanting to know about him and about their father and about anything else Cole was willing to tell her. "What happened?" she asked, her voice barely above a whisper.

◆ ◆ ◆ ◆

Cole let his eyes leave the road long enough for them to focus on Brooke, and he wondered if she could see the pain behind them. He'd never told anyone the truth about what had happened that day, and he wasn't sure he should now either. He'd held it in for over a decade—spent twelve years worrying about what might happen if anyone found out how Brett really died. But now he suddenly didn't care. Maybe it was because he was so far from home or because Brooke had no connection to him or his life other than the short time they'd spent on the road together. Or maybe it was that she was so busy running from her own problems she wouldn't give a shit about his.

Right now, the only thing that mattered was that he felt like if he held it in any longer, his chest might explode under the pressure. "It was my fault," he said quietly after his eyes found the road again. Apparently finding a subtle way to begin the story wasn't possible at that moment. Though logically he knew he wasn't solely responsible for his brother's death, Cole needed to say that sentence to someone more than he realized—like the weight of it was suddenly too much to carry now that he had the chance to put it down. And though his confession wasn't the whole truth, the guilt he'd endured over his inaction that night made it true enough.

He didn't look at Brooke because he was fearful of what he might see in her face or hear if he gave her the opportunity to speak.

So he kept talking. "My dad was an asshole. *Is* an asshole," he corrected. "My mom died when I was four and Brett was seven. The memories I have of her are foggy, like some kinda dream I know I had but can't quite remember. I do remember the funeral, though," he said. "My dad drinking more that morning than I'd ever seen him drink in a whole day, him sobbing like a baby into the casket before the viewing. He didn't know anyone saw him, and I think I was the only one who did."

Cole considered pulling over on the side of the road to have this discussion because somehow it seemed weird to be revealing all this while driving down a highway. But he decided against it. Talking to Brooke about this was hard enough. He didn't want to have to look at her the whole time while he said it. The road was a good distraction.

"You never said anything?" she asked. "Never to Brett or anyone else?"

Cole shook his head. "No. Wouldn't have mattered anyway. I knew right then that things would never be the same again."

Cole rubbed a rough hand over his forehead and then dragged it down his face before letting it settle back onto the cracked leather steering wheel. "My dad always had a temper, but I think my mom was able to get him to keep it in check. Brett always said he had a soft spot for her. And if she got upset when our dad was too hard on us, he'd back off. But without her around, his mean streaks got more frequent. And the alcohol only made things worse. His words turned into the occasional shove, and then..." He sighed heavily before continuing. "Then every argument turned physical."

"You guys were so young," Brooke said. "I'm sorry. I don't mean to make it worse."

"It's fine. It was a long time ago." He wished the assurance he gave Brooke made him feel better too, but he knew it wouldn't. No amount of time and—now he was realizing—distance could repair the damage his dad had done. "We both tried to stay on his good side, but it was impossible. If he lost a job, it was our fault. If he stumbled walking down the steps because he'd been drinkin', it was our fault. *Everything* was our fault."

Brooke was silent, and he couldn't blame her. There wasn't much to say about his fucked-up life. Some of Cole's close friends knew how violent his dad could get, but few knew the full extent of his rage.

"Once Brett was a teenager, he joined the football team and started working out. He got bigger. And when he could start fighting back, he did. Especially when our dad laid a hand on *me*. Brett always got annoyed with me, but that didn't change the fact that I was still his little brother, and he did whatever he could to protect me. Anyway, the night he died, my dad had come home from the bar, or wherever the hell he'd been, to find the kitchen a mess. I mean, it was always a mess with three guys living there, but Brett had made dinner for himself and me, and the spaghetti sauce had boiled over and gotten all over the stove. I'd said I'd clean everything up since Brett had cooked, but I forgot. I went outside to play and then watched TV and fell asleep. I was twelve years old, but I still should've known better."

Cole caught a glimpse of Brooke, and she looked like she wanted to say something but ultimately decided against it. "When my dad got home, he started yellin' about how we had no respect for everything he worked to get us and a bunch of other shit. When he said our mom would've been disappointed in us, I jumped out of bed. I'm not even sure what I was gonna do. But I knew I couldn't just lie there and let him bring her into that."

Cole thought he saw Brooke's muscles tense, as if her body was bracing itself for what she was about to hear.

"My dad got in my face and told me to sit back down before he made me. That was when Brett jumped up to get between us. Sometimes my dad would back down when Brett got involved, because he was a coward. I was an easier target since I was smaller, and I don't think he wanted to actually do anything to seriously hurt Brett since he was the starting quarterback for his high school. He was only a sophomore, and he was better than a lot of the seniors. That was always the one source of pride for my dad where Brett was concerned."

Cole shook his head and breathed deeply before continuing. "Anyway, it all happened so fast—my dad pushing Brett and Brett punching him in the stomach hard enough to make him fall. Our dad's a big guy, but Brett was strong, and my dad was already swaying from drinking all day." The images flashed through Cole's mind like a movie reel on loop. "The two went back and forth, pushing and swinging at each other while I sat curled up in my bed like a scared little kid."

"You *were* a little kid," Brooke said.

"Physically, yeah. But mentally I should've been tougher. I should've been brave enough to help when my dad finally got a few solid punches in. When Brett hit his head on the corner of the night stand and fell to the floor, my dad hit him a few more times to make sure he didn't get back up anytime soon."

Brooke gasped audibly. "Oh, my God."

Cole remembered the last time he saw his brother's eyes open. They were glassy and covered in a thick red from his bloody nose running down his cheeks and onto the pile of dirty clothes he'd landed on. Brett had wiped it away a few times himself, and then Cole had tried to clean him up with a clean T-shirt. "Before he left the room, my dad said to leave Brett there. That he would be fine and he needed to learn a little respect. I should've gone to my neighbors' house and told someone or called the police anyway. But I was scared of what my dad would do to me if I got the authorities involved." Cole hated how selfish that made him sound, but it was a truth he couldn't deny any longer. He'd let Brett suffer so *he* wouldn't have to.

"The most I could bring myself to do was somehow get him into his bed and cover him. I figured letting him go to sleep would do him some good. I had no idea it would have the opposite effect."

"You couldn't have known," Brooke said, placing a hand on his thigh to comfort him.

"I know. But that doesn't change the fact that I could've done something and made the decision not to." After that, he'd made a promise to himself that never again would he stand by and do nothing when he could do *some*thing. "Eventually both of us fell asleep."

Finally, Cole allowed a few tears to fall, and he was thankful that a stream of them didn't follow. "The next morning my dad had no choice but to call 9-1-1. He told the police that Brett came home late after a few kids from a rival school had jumped him."

"They believed that?" Brooke sounded disgusted.

Nodding, he sighed heavily. "It's happened before, so it wasn't surprising. Just said he came home with a bloody nose and stuff and didn't want to talk about it so he let him just go to bed. My dad didn't have any visible injuries, and I was too scared not to corroborate my dad's story. The police looked into the case a little, but without any idea who'd jumped him or where it happened, there wasn't a whole lot they could do. And even though my dad caused it, Brett's death hit him hard. He was still his son. Add some guilt on top of that, and my dad was pretty messed up from it. So the police didn't really have reason to think my dad had anything to do with his death. The autopsy showed Brett had internal bleeding in his brain."

"I'm so sorry," Brooke said, and Cole wondered if he'd said too much, put too much on Brooke before she was ready to hear it.

"Thanks," Cole said. And he meant it. He'd needed to let go of the weight he'd been shouldering for far too long. And though thinking about all of it had been painful, the relief he'd felt after sharing it made it worth it. "I know you said you hate walkin' around worrying about somebody recognizin' you, people thinkin' they know you when all they really know are things *about* you."

Brooke nodded and gave him a quiet "Yeah."

"I can't pretend I know what that's like," Cole continued. "Because no matter how hard I try, I can never seem to be more than the son of a town drunk and the baby brother of a dead star quarterback. I joined the army thinkin' it'd make my life matter, make *me* matter. Like I'd somehow be able to fix some of the shit that's wrong with the world even though I couldn't even fix my own life." He shook his head, disappointed in how naïve he'd been. "But after all the shit I've been through and all the shit I've seen, all I feel is smaller. Like I'm an ant, and any second somethin' so much bigger than me is gonna come up on me and squash everything I know without a second's warning. You know what I mean?"

Brooke nodded again. "I think I do."

A few quiet moments passed before Cole found the words he'd been searching for, and he hoped like hell they were the right ones. "The other day you told me you couldn't stand bein' somebody, and you got mad when I couldn't get that." Cole pulled off the highway toward the hotel. "I've been tryin' to get where you're coming from, Brooke. I really have. I'm tryin' to understand what it'd feel like for people to care about every word I say and every move I make. But honestly, I don't think I'll ever get it. Not fully anyway. Because even though I agree all of that would probably suck, I'll never really know what it's like to be somebody. Not when I've been nobody my whole life."

He hadn't meant to let all of that out like he had, and the fact that Brooke hadn't spoken more than a few words almost made him regret telling her everything. This time he let the silence fill the space between them as he wondered what she was thinking. Did she think his family was trash and that *he* was trash by association? Did she think he was calling her spoiled or pretentious because she was running from something most people run *toward*? Both of those possibilities seemed likely, and Cole hoped that in his effort to bring them closer he hadn't driven them further apart.

"Thank you," she said quietly as Cole turned into the hotel parking lot and killed the engine.

"For what?"

"For all of it. For telling me about what happened to Brett and about what kind of person your dad is." She massaged the skin between her thumb and finger as she spoke. She hadn't been looking at him, instead fixing her eyes on the neon OFFICE sign ahead of them. Finally, she settled her hands on her lap, and her mind seemed to settle with them. When she turned toward him, she looked peaceful. "For the stuff about not wanting to be somebody."

"That may have come out wrong."

She shook her head. "It can't be wrong if I needed to hear it. I have a lot I should be thankful for."

Cole tried to smile at her, but he knew it looked forced. "Yeah, well...so does everyone," he said. "Don't be too hard on yourself. Not when so many other people are happy to do that *for* you." He hoped the last comment might help to lighten the mood.

"'Kay," she replied. And then, "So Arches Park tomorrow?"

Cole gave her a nod and then reached over and squeezed her hand, thinking about how tomorrow was never promised to anyone.

CHAPTER TWELVE

Lying on her back, Brooke inhaled deeply and debated whether to open her eyes. Cole had been running his hand over her body—which was still naked from last night—for at least five minutes. It had started innocently enough. A gentle dragging of his fingertips across her skin while he lay next to her, and then his strong hands kneading the muscles in her thighs, arms, and shoulders once he could sense she was awake.

Her soft moans while he massaged her were what caused him to pull her against him and hold her hips in place so her ass pressed perfectly against his cock. Then he brought a hand up to brush her hair off her neck so he could kiss it. "You feel what you do to me?" he rasped as he ground against her but didn't allow her to move. It turned her on even more than she already was.

"I felt what I do to you three times last night," she said, causing Cole to nip her ear. "I don't even know how you can be hard again."

He released a hand from her hip enough to swirl a finger lightly over her clit. She tried to move against him, but he held her in place. "I've had you naked sleeping next to me all night. How could I *not* be hard?"

It was a valid point, but she was having trouble coming

up with any type of coherent reply with him touching her like he was. His finger moved in delicious circles over her clit, and every so often, he'd dip a finger inside her enough to make the ache deep within her nearly unbearable. Finally, she was able to force out an "I need to come," and the plea made him laugh softly into her ear.

"I think we both need that," he replied. "But I actually don't have any condoms left."

He dipped his hips lower so he could slip his cock between her thighs and rub against her. God, she wanted to tell him to forget the condom and fuck her senseless until they both exploded with their need for each other. But she knew that would be a reckless decision. Not that most of her recent decisions would be considered sensible—skipping out on a contract, trekking across the country with no plan in place, and then finally hitching a ride with a stranger. Her actions hadn't exactly screamed "safe and responsible," yet somehow trusting her instincts had worked out so far. And though all her instincts told her to hop onto Cole's dick, she just couldn't bring herself to do it. She certainly didn't think of Cole as a stranger anymore, but he was when it came to his sexual history. "Well, I guess we'll have to get creative, then."

Cole groaned so low into the crook of her neck, she felt the vibration down her spine. "What'd you have in mind?"

The truth was she didn't have anything in mind. She liked what they were doing right now—the way Cole's thrusts between her thighs teased her in exactly the right way, how thick and smooth he felt. "I'm liking this," she said.

Cole didn't reply but instead sped up his long strokes

with his cock. She wished it were inside her, but this still felt so good. Especially when she angled herself in a way that allowed the head of his dick to rub over her clit with every stroke. She tightened her thighs around him, giving them both more friction, and the sharp breath Cole exhaled when she did it told her it was appreciated. His fingers were still on her clit, but his touch was light—slow circles and gentle taps that had her pressing his hand down harder with her own. She felt him smile against her neck and let out a low laugh. She guessed the bastard had been waiting for her to do that, probably enjoying watching her squirm with need while he gave her just enough to drive her crazy but not enough to get her off.

Cole followed her lead, moving his hand exactly as hers guided him to. All of it felt so fucking good. Until Cole slid his hand out from under hers.

"What are you doing?" she practically choked out.

Instead of answering, he placed his hand over hers, pressing her own fingers over herself. The pressure alone was practically enough to make her come, so she moved her hips to grind against her fingers.

"Touch yourself," Cole said.

Wasn't she doing that already? "I am."

"No. I mean touch yourself like you do when no one's watching."

"Cole...I don't..."

He slowed his thrusts, dragging his cock too slowly against her slick entrance. "Everyone does it, Princess," he said after a kiss to her shoulder blade. "Even you."

She huffed but didn't remove her hand from herself. "Not

with people in the room."

"I'm not 'people.' And besides, if anyone's used to having an audience, it's you," he said.

Smartass.

"You were the one who said to get creative," he said. Then he moved his fingers from over her hand up to her stomach and then to her nipple. "Do you want to come or not?"

Cole hadn't ever shown this side of himself before, but she had to admit she liked it. The realization that he wanted her to do something so intimate with him right there made the whole thing even hotter. And to answer his question, yes, she wanted to come. Really fucking badly.

So with Cole's hands roving over her body and his thick cock moving between her legs, she touched herself. Softly at first until she couldn't help but give herself more, she brought herself closer and closer to orgasm. "I'm gonna come," she said. But before the sentence had fully left her lips, she was already letting go. A few seconds later, Cole followed, his cock spurting long bursts of come onto her hand, which she'd moved down over his tip so she could feel his release.

She could feel Cole's chest moving up and down against her back, their breaths almost synchronized. They hadn't even kissed or looked at each other. Yet, somehow it was one of the most intimate sexual encounters she'd ever had. She wasn't sure what would happen between the two of them after they got to Oregon, but right now she didn't want to think about it. Cole was by her side, holding her tightly. It meant she was safe, protected, happy. For now, anyway.

♦ ♦ ♦ ♦

By the time they'd managed to drag themselves out of bed and wake up enough to take showers and dress, it was nearing eleven thirty. But it was also already ninety-eight degrees and projected to get even hotter by the height of the day. Though it had still been hot yesterday, the temperature hadn't been quite as high. And it had been partly cloudy, making it feel a little cooler than it was. He'd still be happy to go to Arches today if Brooke wanted to go, but he felt he should give her fair warning. "It's pretty hot today," he said.

She looked over at him from where she was standing in front of the mirror fixing her hair. "It's pretty hot *every* day."

Cole laughed as he pulled a T-shirt over his head. "True. But it's worse than yesterday. It'll probably be above a hundred soon. I was thinkin' it might be too hot for Arches, but if you wanna go, I'm game."

Brooke's lips twisted in thought. "I did want to go. But that is really hot. I wouldn't want to have to drive your ass to the hospital if you pass out or something."

He couldn't resist. "Scared someone'll recognize you and ask for your autograph?"

She chucked some sort of hair stuff at him she'd been using and then gave him a shove to his broad chest with both hands.

The fact that he fell back onto the bed definitely had more to do with him wanting to play along than it did her strength. Once on the bed, he pulled her onto him so she was straddling his hips.

"So if we didn't go to the park, what would we do today? I can't bear the thought of driving another eight hours to Yellowstone today. And it's already past checkout, so we're paying for another night regardless."

Cole ran his hands up and down her sides and then over her ass to massage it under her shorts. "I'm sure we can think of something," he said.

She gave him an exaggerated eye roll. But the way her gaze settled back on him told him she was more interested than she let on. "We can't just stay in this room all day and have sex."

"Says who?"

"Says me. And you, actually," she added. "Didn't you say you were out of condoms?"

"Oh yeah."

"Well, let's drive into whatever town we're near and get pancakes and condoms. I'm starving."

Cole couldn't help but laugh at her words. They were on the exact same page.

After finding a drugstore, they settled into a table at a nearby café. The waitress brought them each a glass of water, and when they ordered coffee, she was back within seconds. "Fresh pot," she said, putting down the porcelain cups and saucers and filling them almost to the brim. She told them she'd give them a few minutes to decide, and she'd be back to take their orders shortly.

When she returned, she set down a plate of pastries between them—some sort of apple walnut cinnamon bread and a few mini danishes. Cole wasn't sure why it hadn't ever occurred to him that restaurants never put out something before breakfast like they did with rolls or bread at other meals, but now that he'd seen a place do it, he didn't think he could ever go back.

After the waitress took their order, they dug into their little appetizer plate. "You getting excited to get to Oregon?" Brooke asked.

"Excited" wasn't exactly what Cole was feeling, but he *did* want to get there. Though truthfully less than he had before he'd met Brooke. Cole picked up his napkin from his lap and wiped his face so he didn't have to answer right away. Nodding, he tried to think of a response that wasn't a lie. "It's been a while since I've seen Jimmy."

"You guys have any big plans or anything?"

"Nope. Are you plannin' to come all the way to Oregon, or were you wantin' to head somewhere else?"

"I'll ride with you all the way if that's cool with you." She poured a little more cream in her coffee. "I promise not to intrude on your guys' weekend or whatever."

"And after Oregon?" he asked. He wanted to steer the conversation away from Jimmy, and that was the next logical question. Plus, it was something he'd been wondering about the last few days. As far as he was concerned, what he had with Brooke was more than just casual sex that filled a need while he was on the road.

Brooke stopped stirring her coffee and put down the spoon, looking across at him intently before she spoke. "Guess we can figure that out together," she said.

And it was exactly what Cole needed to hear.

CHAPTER THIRTEEN

"I can't believe you talked me into this," Cole said as they entered the resort.

"I can," Brooke said simply, a small smile threatening to creep over her lips. "I think behind that manly exterior you're a metrosexual at heart."

Cole turned so he was facing her completely. "We're not getting manicures or somethin' while we're here, are we? The fact that the word 'spa' is in the name scares me a little."

Brooke stared ahead at the couple in front of them who were checking in. "I haven't booked our spa appointments yet, so anything's possible."

Before Cole had a chance to respond, the couple moved to the side with their bags, which were much larger and clearly nicer than what Brooke and Cole had brought inside.

"Good afternoon," the woman said with a welcoming smile. "How can I help you today?"

"We'd like to check in," Brooke told her.

"Certainly. Can I have the last name on the reservation, please?"

"We don't actually have one," Brooke replied. "But I called last night, and the person I spoke to said there were rooms available for tonight and tomorrow."

The woman tapped her fingers against the computer keys rapidly before looking back up at Brooke. "We do. So you're planning a two-night stay, you said?"

Brooke nodded.

"Perfect. We can certainly help you. I'll just need a credit card and ID, and I'll be happy to take care of you."

Brooke hesitated, her eyes darting to Cole, who was a few feet away looking at a brochure he'd grabbed from a nearby rack. She thought about asking for his credit card and telling him she'd give him the money if it came to that.

"I was planning to pay in cash," Brooke said.

"That's perfectly fine. We won't put the room on your card. It's just to hold it. You can pay your bill in cash when you check out."

"Can I just pay for it in advance?" Brooke knew this was a stretch, and she probably should have anticipated they'd ask for a credit card, but she'd lucked out so far and had hoped that luck would hold out.

The woman's shake of her head made it clear her lucky streak was over. "I'm sorry. That's against policy."

Stalling for a second, Brooke quickly mulled over her options. She had kept one card on her in case of emergencies. This didn't qualify as an emergency, but she also didn't want to needlessly cause an issue.

"Nothing will be charged to it, right?" Brooke asked.

"No ma'am. The card is simply a precaution in the event that there is significant damage to the room or if you don't pay at checkout."

Brooke couldn't help feeling anxious, but she knew it was

standard procedure, so she handed the woman a card. A few minutes later, they were in their room, a small rustic space made mostly of wood—from the walls to the bed frame.

Cole ran his hand over the bed post, which looked like a thin log. Then he knocked twice on it. "This place is actually pretty nice," he said. He tossed his bag on the bed and sat beside it, bouncing up and down slightly. "Bed seems solid." He raised an eyebrow at her before reaching out to pull her toward him.

"What do you have planned for the weekend, Princess? This place has a ton of stuff to do. We can rent ATVs or fish."

He sounded so hopeful, she already felt bad. But there was no way she was doing either one of those things. "Both of those sound too dangerous."

Cole's eyes narrowed. "How is fishing dangerous?"

"It's boring as hell, and I'm worried I might try to off myself with a rusty hook."

Cole's expression softened, and there was a sadness to it that made her wonder if she'd insulted his pastime even more than she'd meant to. "I'm kidding. I'm sure fishing's fun. For some people," she added. "I've just never been into that type of thing. I was thinking since we did some hiking and other outdoorsy type things on our trip so far, I could switch it up a bit...show you some things I like. Like sunrise yoga...or a couple's massage."

She expected Cole to protest immediately, but he didn't seem to be listening. His eyes seemed to be looking past her at something that wasn't even there. He was probably more tired than she'd even realized.

"Did you hear me?" She squatted down so she was at eye

level with him. "I said we can paint each other's nails and then hit up some designer outlets."

He seemed to come back to himself with a start. "Sorry," he said with a quick shake of his head. "Yeah, I heard you. No way I'm painting my nails. Or lettin' you paint 'em either. I gotta draw the line somewhere."

He gave her a smile that reassured her more than she realized she needed. "So that's a yes to the massage, yoga, and shopping, then?"

Cole smacked her ass with a sharp sting. "Don't push your luck, Princess. I still have a reputation I gotta uphold."

"I wouldn't worry about it. I don't think anyone will mistake you for anything other than a shaggy-haired, rugged Southern charmer who's only at a place like this because his girl dragged him here."

"Good," Cole said more seriously than the moment called for. Then he tickled her hips and gave her a soft kiss on the lips before saying, "Let's go find this spa you keep talking about."

◆ ◆ ◆ ◆

The last thing Cole Timmons ever thought he'd be doing was lying outside on a massage table next to a beautiful singer while some man with muscles bigger than Cole's dug his hands into Cole's back. But that was exactly what he found himself doing, and he didn't regret anything about it.

Well, maybe one thing. Since he didn't like the idea of Thor's younger brother putting his hands all over Brooke, Cole had requested the male massage therapist. When Brooke had looked at him strangely, he'd given some explanation about how his back and shoulders were killing him from the long drive, and a guy would probably be rougher and harder than a woman would. As soon as he'd said the words, he'd realized his mistake. Brooke had looked at him for a moment as she held in the laughter he knew would burst out of her at any moment. And soon enough, they were both in a fit of hysterics in the spa lobby.

Once he'd pulled it together enough to speak, he'd admitted the real reason for his request. And since Brooke didn't exactly like the idea of a beautiful masseuse touching Cole either, she agreed to take the woman.

"I could get used to this," Cole said, his head rolling to the side so he could look at Brooke on the table next to him. The air was somehow refreshing despite the heat of the day, and Cole could see the sun about to set in the distance. Between that and Brooke's partially undressed body beside him, it was, without a doubt, the most perfect sight Cole had ever laid eyes on.

"Told you," she said with a small smile. Her eyes were still closed as Cole watched her. It was the most relaxed either of them had been in a long time, and he didn't want it to ever end. "Better than fishing, isn't it?"

The comment made Cole chuckle. "Maybe a little."

This time Brooke opened her eyes and let them settle on Cole. "I'm gonna miss this," she said.

Cole knew she was talking about having to give up life's luxuries if she decided not to continue with her music. But he couldn't help but let himself think it had a deeper meaning than that. "Me too," he said quietly.

After they finished their spa treatments, they took a shower, which somehow stayed relatively innocent save for running soap over each other's skin. Then they ordered room service and spent the rest of the evening outside with only a bottle of wine and each other. When they finally crawled into bed, they were both too tired to do anything but sleep. But his exhaustion didn't stop Cole from having the nightmare he'd thought he'd moved past.

He hadn't dreamed about that day in almost a year, and though he wanted to tell himself he didn't know the reason for the dream, he knew that wasn't true. He'd be in Oregon in only a few short days. Cole flipped over to look at the time on his phone. *Not even five yet.* He knew he should go back to sleep, but since he also knew he wouldn't be able to, he decided he'd do the next best thing: watch the sun rise.

He dressed quickly and left the hotel room as quietly as he could. Just because he was up didn't mean that Brooke needed to be. Especially since this was something he felt he should do alone. The last time he'd seen a sunrise had been overseas when he and a buddy or two were on watch. The sunrise meant cigarettes and celebration because they'd survived another night—lived to see another day. And that meant something.

Before enlisting, he'd never been up early enough to watch the sun come up. And after his deployment, he hadn't thought there was any reason to. Most days, especially when he'd first come home, he hadn't wanted to get out of bed at all. He didn't give a shit that it was a new day or a blank slate or any of the clichés people told themselves to give them a reason to keep going. Because when it came down to it, each day was like the last and none of them felt worth living. Especially when not everyone got the opportunity to live them at all.

He'd lost more than friends over there. He'd lost his motivation and drive. He'd lost a part of himself he hadn't even realized he had until he didn't seem to have it anymore. Cole couldn't remember a darker time in his life than the first few months after he'd come home. Few people had given a shit when he'd left, and even fewer cared when he'd come back. That was when he'd realized that the world kept turning, and other people's lives had continued during his absence. It made him feel more disconnected from his life in Georgia than he had before he'd left.

And it brought him into a hole so dark he wasn't sure he could climb out of it. There was only one reason he hadn't made the choice to end all of it. He had exactly that: a choice. It was something so many of his friends—his *family*—hadn't been given. The decision had been made *for* them without their consent or the protest of their loved ones. None of them had gotten the opportunity to decide when and how their lives would end. And Cole sure as hell wasn't special enough to get that privilege when so many better men hadn't.

Jimmy would have kicked his ass if Cole had given up. Which was why Cole was driving across the country to Oregon. He owed it to Jimmy to thank him in person.

But now he realized Jimmy wasn't the only thing that kept him moving forward anymore. And as Cole watched the first ray of light rise in the distance, he finally felt that there was an even stronger reason to keep going, a reason to actually give a shit about his future.

And that reason was sound asleep inside his hotel room.

CHAPTER FOURTEEN

Brooke was still asleep when Cole went back inside, but he was too awake to join her. Instead, he grabbed his phone and wallet from the table, slipped them quietly inside the pocket of his jeans, and headed back outside. There was a small café in the lobby, and Cole wanted to pick up some coffee and pastries.

The resort was expansive, acres of greenery with stone paths connecting the strips of hotel rooms and villas, and he found himself walking more slowly than he intended to as he took in his surroundings. At the café, he ordered an assortment of danishes and donuts—which he was sure he'd eat most of— and some sort of apple cinnamon cake that he thought Brooke would like. He tossed some creamers and sugar packets into the carrier with the coffees and headed back outside.

He wasn't sure what Brooke had planned for the day, but whatever it was, he was sure he'd enjoy it. He understood now why so many people took weekend getaways to places like this if they could afford it. He'd only been here a day, and he already felt rejuvenated in a way he never thought possible.

"Excuse me," a voice called from a few feet away. Cole turned to see a middle-aged man leaning against a silver sedan. He held a map in his hand and went back to studying it after Cole turned toward him. "I'm trying to find the smaller hot spring pools. The large ones are closed for cleaning apparently."

Normally, Cole would have been happy to help, but something about this guy put Cole on guard. His face held the hard sternness of a person in law enforcement or military, and in khakis and a short-sleeve dress shirt, he didn't look like he was dressed to go swimming. "I think they're about fifty yards that way," Cole said, pointing in the opposite direction of the man. "But I've only been here a day, so I haven't been to them yet."

The man looked at the map and then back at the surrounding buildings. "Trying to get my bearings," he said. "I'm horrible with directions. Do you even know where we are on this thing?"

Cole moved toward the man and glanced at the map. "The blue building is the one behind us right here. I think the pools you're asking about are past it."

"Thank you," he said, folding the map carefully and setting it on the top of the trunk before sliding his hands into his pockets and looking at Cole appraisingly. "You enjoying your time with her, Mr. Timmons?"

"Excuse me?" The man's question had done more than surprise Cole. It made him stand up straighter.

Cole was at least three inches taller than this guy and in better shape, but the way this man carried himself told Cole he would be close to an equal match if they were to fight. "I asked if you were enjoying your time with Brooke."

Cole's jaw went rigid, but he loosened it enough to speak. "Who are you?" he asked before setting down the drinks and bag of pastries on the trunk of a car next to him.

"No, Mr. Timmons, the question is who are *you*? Not that you need to answer that. I already know all I need to about you. And none of it's impressive."

Cole stepped as close to the man as he could without touching him. "You should leave."

"Brooke's got commitments. And none of them involve *you*."

Cole was starting to wonder if this motherfucker *wanted* to get hit. "What do you care what she does? You her father or somethin'?"

"No," the man answered, and his voice seemed to soften enough to make Cole wonder how he could be so casual about something so serious. He'd clearly come a long way to say all this. "But her dad sent me. Both her parents did, actually. They're worried about her. And I am too. I've been her bodyguard since she was a teenager. I wouldn't make a trip like this for just anybody."

"Well, you shouldn't have bothered. She's fine. Brooke's a big girl. She can take care of herself."

"Can she?"

Cole let the question hover between them before blowing out a puff of air through his nose in disgust. "She's still alive, right?"

The man nodded calmly. "She is. And she has you to thank for that."

"What the fuck, man? First you come here tellin' me to leave the girl alone, and now you're tellin' me she should be thankin' me? Which is it?" Cole allowed him a few seconds to answer, and when he didn't, Cole brought a finger up to point in the man's face. "You know what? Forget it. I don't give a shit what you have to say anymore."

He turned to walk away but didn't get far before the man spoke again. "You her boyfriend or her bodyguard? Because one she already has, and the other you don't quite have the résumé for."

"Fuck you," Cole called without turning around. "You got no idea what you're talkin' about."

"No? Because it seems to me the only thing you know how to do is run from your problems and create more."

Cole knew he shouldn't give this guy the satisfaction of a response, but he couldn't help it. He'd be damned if he was gonna let this...stranger act like he knew anything about him other than his name. "I don't create more problems," he said after turning back around to face him.

"Maybe not for yourself. But Brooke's got a slew of them right now—starting with the fact that she has a televised performance she needs to attend in a few days and a tour contract she needs to sign."

"She doesn't wanna do either of those."

"You speak for her now too?" the man countered. "Because the last time I checked, you weren't her agent. You're just some backwoods boy with a chip on his shoulder and something to prove. You think you're helping her by taking her farther away from home, from the life she and her family built? Just because your life's worth leaving doesn't mean hers is too."

Cole told himself to calm down. He told himself to unclench his fists and walk away. Because staring at this dude any longer would only result in Cole hitting him. And that was exactly what the guy was trying to prove by telling Cole that he was some lowlife fucking redneck who was ruining Brooke's life simply by being with her. The fact that there was an element of truth to it didn't make it any easier to take. "Fuck you," Cole spat before heading toward their room.

"Tell her I'm waiting for her when she's ready," the man called after him.

And though it was a small one, the fact that he hadn't gone back to deck the guy somehow felt like a victory.

◆ ◆ ◆ ◆

At the sound of the door opening, Brooke looked up from the magazine she'd been reading. "Where'd *you* run off to this morning?" she asked. "I was lonely."

"I went to get coffee."

"Aww, and you didn't even bring me any back?" She thought that was a little odd, especially since he didn't have a coffee for himself either but reasoned he must have finished it before he returned.

Cole shrugged and then put his keys on the round, wooden table near the door. Then he took a seat in the chair beside it. "Sorry. You didn't say you wanted any."

"In my defense, I was asleep when you left. And just so you know, in the future it's always safe to assume I want coffee."

Cole rubbed his hands together, keeping his eyes fixed on them rather than looking up. "'Kay."

"You all right? You don't really seem yourself," she said.

Cole's lips twisted for a moment before he opened them

to speak. "Who am I?"

"What?"

"You said I don't seem like myself, so I was just wondering who I am."

"Why are you acting like this?"

Cole shook his head before pressing his palms to his thighs and standing. "I'm not *acting* like anything."

"Okay," she said slowly. "If you say so."

"You've known me for what? About a week? And suddenly you're an expert on every little detail about me?"

The abrasiveness of his words silenced her for longer than she wanted to be. "I'd like to think I know you, yeah. We've spent every second together since we met. You told me things no one else knows."

"Don't talk about that."

"We don't have to talk about it. I'm *not* talking about it. I'm trying to show you that I know you better than you're giving me credit for." She had no idea what was wrong with him, but regardless of what Cole said, she knew one thing for sure—this wasn't the person she'd spent the last...however many days with.

Cole rubbed his hands through his hair. "If you know so much, then you'd know that I'm the kind of guy who cuts and runs when shit gets complicated. And this"—he gestured between them—"is way fucking complicated."

"You can't be serious." Brooke hated how her voice broke on the last syllable. Hated she was showing him he was hurting her.

"Your bodyguard is downstairs. He said he'll wait for you."

Cole began moving around the room, gathering his stuff.

Brooke put her hand on his arm to stop him. "Wait, what? Dean is here?"

"He didn't give me his name. But if a big guy with a shaved head and a bad attitude is Dean, then yes. I ran into him downstairs." Cole pulled away from her and continued packing.

Brooke stared at him for a second. For the first time in a week, she felt like she was looking at a stranger. "So that's it? I tell you how I feel about going back to that life, and this is what you do?"

"I told you. Shit was fucked up when I was a kid so I enlisted the first chance I got. Then shit in the army went south so I quit. Life in Georgia sucked so I took off again. See the theme, Princess?"

"You didn't abandon me when I needed you at that gas station or at the bar. Why are you doing it now?"

He dropped his bag and faced her. "Because you don't belong with me. I have nothing, but you have a whole life waiting for you. You belong in the world while all I want to do is exist on the fringe of it. This was nothing more than a stop on one of your tours. Not a destination."

Brooke disagreed. She felt they clicked in every way that truly mattered. Her life back home was superficial. The past week had been filled with adventure and depth and feeling.

They hadn't talked about what would happen after Oregon, but the fact that they'd said they'd discuss it had given Brooke hope that she might mean more to him than just some traveling partner. And she mentally scolded herself for allowing herself to have hope of something more—hope Cole was squashing with every passing word. She wanted to tell him their lives weren't as different as he thought they were, that they could make it work between them if they both wanted it badly enough. But she didn't say any of that. How could she when he was packing his shit and bailing on her? "Maybe you're right" was all she could get out without her voice cracking with the tears she felt threatening to fall.

Without looking at her, Cole picked up his bag. "It's probably best if I go now," he said. "No point in dragging this out any more than it needs to be. I can call you a cab to take you to a train station or something if you don't want to head back with your bodyguard."

"Don't do me any more favors," she said. "Just go."

He hesitated for only a second before he went to the door and pulled it open. "For what it's worth, I will miss you."

She stared him down, willing the tears away. "Well, I'll be on *What's Up, America?* in about a week. You could tune in and get a glimpse of the life that, according to you, I'm meant to be living."

Cole didn't reply right away, and the silence that stretched between them was oppressive. Finally, he said a soft, "Goodbye, Brooke," and was gone.

It wasn't until a few seconds after the door closed that she allowed the dam she'd built behind her eyes to collapse. And with every tear that fell, she tried desperately to rid herself of the man she was sure she'd never forget.

CHAPTER FIFTEEN

"Brookey, are you ready?"

Her mother's singsongy voice was like nails on a chalkboard, even muffled through her bedroom door. There were few things Brooke hated more than when her mom called her "Brookey." It made her feel like a five-year-old, which was actually probably appropriate since that was also how her mom treated her.

"Almost."

"Well, try to hurry. Arthur will be here soon."

Brooke heard a creak in the hall, which meant her mother had walked away from her door. Letting out a deep breath, Brooke looked at her reflection in the vanity. She looked haggard. Her eyes were puffy, her skin pale, even her hair—which her mom had had a conniption about when she'd first seen Brooke—looked flat. It was like every part of her body was expressing a misery that felt bone-deep. Arthur, her lawyer, would probably stroke out when he saw her. He had a lot of money riding on this deal too, after all.

Her parents had so far refused to comment on the sadness that felt so pervasive, Brooke wondered if she'd fallen into a full-fledged depression. They had to notice it, but to comment would have given it wings—made it something that needed to be addressed instead of ignored until it passed.

Brooke didn't think it would ever pass. She was going to spend the next thirty-six months on a world tour she didn't want any part of, her parents would be with her for its entirety, and it would give her worldwide recognition. It was pretty much every nightmare she'd ever had wrapped up into one.

But those things weren't even the worst of it for her. Despite her mind constantly berating her for it, Brooke missed Cole. Terribly, deeply, painfully. He'd cast her aside like she meant nothing to him, but she wasn't able to do the same. Thinking about Cole was somehow like thinking about her brightest day and her worst stomach bug. It was ridiculous. She hardly knew him. They'd spent together what would ultimately be a blip on the reel of her life. But Brooke suspected the memory of him would be stamped on every frame for a long time to come. And she wasn't sure how to handle that along with everything else.

She felt one negative comment away from a mental breakdown, which scared the hell out of her. She wasn't this person. Sure, she'd allowed herself to be walked over by her parents for her entire life, but she didn't let others do it. Sure as hell not strangers. And she especially needed to not let it be done by one who'd picked her up in a gas station, for fuck's sake. Taking a deep breath, Brooke willed herself to slip on the mask she'd been wearing since she was a teenager. The one that made her look like a confident, untouchable professional who didn't get hung up on Southern boys with adorable dimples and worn-in Levi's.

Standing up, she drew her shoulders back and held her head high. She'd have to bury Brooke Alba and become Brooke

Devereaux to pull all of this off. Even though she knew that in doing so, there'd be no going back. The girl she'd been had to die in order for any semblance of herself to live. Brooke opened the door to her room and walked out, knowing full well the life she was walking toward wasn't the better option. But it was the only one.

♦ ♦ ♦ ♦

Cole arrived in the small town in Oregon where Jimmy had grown up as the sun was beginning to go down. Exhaustion had hit him fifty miles ago, but he'd been unable to stop. Getting to Jimmy had been why he'd set out on this trip in the first place, and once he'd gotten close, it was as if that purpose had become a desperate need. Once there, he'd have finished what he'd started. The fact that he'd been sidetracked along the way by a girl he'd sent away even while he knew she'd be taking his heart right along with her was no longer at the forefront of his mind. He'd talk things out with Jimmy. Being with him would put everything else into perspective.

Cole used his phone to search for the name of the place where Jimmy was and followed the directions. It only took ten minutes to get there. He pulled through the wrought-iron gates and continued down the narrow road a bit before pulling over and putting the car in park. With a deep breath, Cole pushed the door open and got out.

He'd had to look around a bit before he found Jimmy's headstone. When he saw it, Cole was hit with a sudden wave of sadness that he hadn't been able to be there for the funeral. Jimmy had been his best friend for almost four years. Not being there had felt all kinds of wrong, but Cole had been deployed, and the choice hadn't been his.

As he read the headstone of Sergeant James Ventura, beloved husband, father, and son, tears welled in Cole's eyes. Losing Jimmy had been like losing a limb for him, so he couldn't even begin to imagine what it must have been like for his family. He'd seen numerous pictures of Jimmy's wife and daughter, but he'd never met any of Jimmy's relatives in person. Judging by the fresh flowers laid on his grave and the pristine American flag that blew in the soft wind, Cole figured they came often.

Squatting down, Cole rubbed a hand over the words on Jimmy's headstone. "Sorry it took me so long to come see ya, buddy. I don't even have a good excuse except I wasn't ready to face you 'til now." Truth was, despite being on his way to visit Jimmy, Cole hadn't let himself think about the man much beyond the memories that surfaced in his nightmares. The image of the truck pulling up with a lifeless Jimmy—his eyes devoid of their usual brightness, his body a battered shell of what it had been—had been riding Cole's subconscious more and more as he'd gotten closer. Not that it should've surprised Cole. Losing Jimmy had been like losing his brother all over again.

"You were always everything I wished I could be. A dedicated soldier, a good son...a great man." Cole let his hands drop and clasped them between his thighs. "I kinda felt like I was becoming those things. A good man at least. But"—Cole shrugged—"just like everything else, I fucked it all up."

The wind blew a little stronger, gusting through Cole's

hair, tousling it. He ducked his head into the breeze as if it were a caress. "You always did like fucking up my hair," he said with a laugh. They'd been mandated to keep it short while deployed, but Cole always bucked the rules a bit, letting it grow out until his CO threatened to hack it off with a chainsaw.

Cole shifted so he was leaning back against Jimmy's headstone, his legs bent in front of him. "I went home after I decided not to re-up. I was hoping my old man would be happy to see me. Maybe even respect me a little. Stupid, huh? All he wanted to know was what I was going to do for work now that I was done playing G.I. Joe." Cole let his head fall forward. "Anyway, I stuck around there longer than I should have. He's an asshole who makes me an asshole too. Packed up what little stuff I had and hit the road to come see you. So here I am."

The sun blazed over a hill in the distance, causing the sky to become streaked with burnt orange and red hues. Cole looked up at it until his vision blurred. It took him a minute to realize he was crying, but once he did, it turned into the kind of body-shuddering sobbing that made it hard to breathe. "What the hell am I gonna do now, Jimmy?" he choked out between sobs.

The reality was, the only plan Cole had had was to make it to Jimmy. He was here. So...now what? Where the hell did he go from here? His skills were wrapped up in being a soldier, but he didn't want to do that anymore. Couldn't do it. Seeing what remained of Jimmy's body after he'd gone on a patrol and run over an IED had broken Cole. Joining the army had been a way for Cole to escape his shitty town and shittier father. But then he'd needed to escape the army, followed by needing to escape the civilian life that made him feel like his skin was too tight. Now there was nowhere else to escape to.

The only time Cole had ever been truly content was when he'd been with Brooke. But just like everything else, he'd ruined it. Granted, he'd done it for her. What the hell did he have to offer someone like her? She deserved better.

Cole got himself under control a bit and turned to look at the headstone again. Jimmy had deserved better too. If there was ever a man who didn't deserve to return home in a box, it was the man whose grave Cole was visiting. "Why can't life ever be fucking fair?" Jimmy had an entire family who'd depended on him. If it had been Cole killed in action, no one would've even missed him. His dad sure as hell wouldn't have come to leave flowers at his gravesite. Jimmy had been loved—was still loved. His absence left a gaping hole in the lives of everyone who knew him.

Kind of like the hole Brooke had left in Cole's life. He wondered if she'd miss him—when she got over hating him, which he was sure she did because he deserved to be hated by her. She'd needed him, trusted him to protect her, and as soon as he'd had to show up for her—not against some prick in a bar but against a threat that was almost as ominous to her—he'd bailed on her.

Beating the hell out of some drunk asshole was easy. But fighting the truth, that he was nothing but a hick who would hold Brooke back, seemed impossible. It was the very thing people had always said about his father after his mom died. "Oh, that poor Mary Timmons. That no-good husband of hers pulled her down. At least now she'll have some peace." Cole didn't want to be that guy.

But as the sun disappeared and the air around him grew crisp, Cole wondered if he had to be that guy. If he was genetically predispositioned to be a screw-up, or if he could be...more. "You always said I could be anything I wanted to be," Cole said to his friend. "But what if I don't know what that is?"

But even as he voiced the words, Cole realized he did know. It had been something that had only been a vague idea to him until two weeks ago, when a beautiful stranger had needed a ride. In the time since, that idea had morphed into a reality that was as complex as it was simple. But now that she was gone, that reality had been ripped away from him, and he didn't think he could ever get it back without her.

Cole sat in the cemetery for hours, trying to figure out how to recapture what he'd lost. He talked through myriad of thoughts that weighed him down and let the ground beneath him absorb them. He gave the doubts over to Jimmy because he knew Jimmy would willingly hold them so Cole could live. Truly live, unencumbered by the things that had held him back from what he wanted the most: to be happy.

And as he stood and said his goodbyes to his best friend, Cole knew he'd be leaving a very different man than the one who had come. If he was being honest with himself, he'd started becoming a new man in that rundown gas station in Kansas. He had his sights set on a future. Now he just had to go get it.

CHAPTER SIXTEEN

"You ready, Ms. Devereaux?"

Brooke's head snapped up to look at the young assistant wearing a headset over her long brown hair. The woman looked harried, which Brooke could relate to. Every cell in Brooke's body jangled with anxiety and maybe even a touch of foreboding. But Brooke knew to keep all of that locked inside. She turned to look at herself in the mirror and saw the reflection of a confident—almost bored—performer. The mask had served her well over the past few days leading up to this event, and Brooke would have been proud of the fact that she hadn't let it slip even a millimeter if she didn't feel as though she were completely lost behind it.

"Yes," she said, her voice deep and strong. "I'm ready." Brooke stood and gave herself one more once-over in the mirror, taking in the shimmering gold micro dress the wardrobe department had given her this morning. It didn't leave much to the imagination, but she figured headlining for pop heartthrob Jacoby Hale necessitated a certain level of sex appeal.

Brooke followed the woman down a long corridor before turning right and walking through a tunnel that would lead them to the stage that was set up outside the *What's Up, America?* studio. Despite having performed countless times before, this was the first time Brooke would be aired live on a major network. It was almost ten a.m., the time Brooke was set to perform one of the new singles she'd recorded before disappearing into the Midwest with Cole.

Cole.

The thought of him caused a knot to form in the pit of her stomach. She'd been home for nearly a week, but the pain from knowing she'd never see him again was still almost unbearable. She'd done her best to tell herself it didn't matter—*he* didn't matter—but it was all bullshit. The more accurate truth was that nothing mattered *without* him. Brooke had no doubt that if he hadn't rejected her, she'd be in a very different place right then. Likely somewhere in Oregon having lunch with Cole's old army buddy and his wife. If he had a wife. Brooke had never thought to ask, and the knowledge of that made her heart hurt even worse. She'd asked so few questions, known so little about the man who'd become so important to her.

His sending her away had hurt, but she also knew it wasn't fair to blame him for falling back into her life as though she hadn't taken off a few weeks ago without a word. The mistake she was about to make was all on her. And she wasn't going to do a damn thing to stop it because ultimately, she had nothing else. She couldn't be who she wanted—didn't even know who that was really—so she'd be who everyone else wanted her to be and hope that one day her priorities would shift to match her parents' dream.

She heard the hosts of *What's Up, America?* talking to the crowd, hyping them up for her performance even though most of them probably had only the vaguest ideas of who she was.

After they fitted her with her mic, Brooke closed her eyes and took a few deep breaths. She let herself get lost in her mind for a moment, and she found herself transported to the Rockies, standing on the side of the road and looking over at Cole as he smiled that breathtaking smile. She wished she could see it for real, even if it was only one more time.

A gentle nudge startled her. "You're on," the assistant whispered.

Brooke must have missed them calling her name, but the roar of the crowd was enough of a clue that she was up. People were always so supportive on things like this, even if they weren't familiar with the artist performing. They got caught up in the energy of the moment and let themselves get carried away by it. Brooke wished she could do the same. Instead, she felt like she was going to puke all over her gold Gucci shoes.

Taking one more deep breath, she climbed the short set of steps and walked onto the stage with a big wave and an even bigger smile. The hosts welcomed her with hugs and air kisses.

"It's so great to see you again," Danica Reynolds, the female host said, even though Brooke had never met her before this moment. "I just love your new album."

"Thank you so much. I'm so proud of this album and can't wait to share it with everyone," Brooke replied with the fakest smile she'd ever mustered.

"We can't wait to hear a song from it today," said the co-host, Brad Turner. "And we also heard you have some big news to share with us."

Brooke had to gulp past the lump that had formed in her throat. "I just might," she teased.

"Well then, we better get out of the way and let you perform so you can share your news with us," Danica squealed in a way that was unbecoming of anyone over the age of eight.

Brooke smiled again as they walked offstage, leaving her standing there alone to take in the immense crowd in front of her. Brooke had always felt butterflies before she performed, but it wasn't ever anything she couldn't handle. Ultimately, singing had started off as something fun, and when it had grown more serious, Brooke typically cared so little about the future of it she didn't feel any kind of overwhelming anxiety. But today, there was a deeper emotional well inside of her that felt like it was close to bubbling over.

Her band struck the familiar chord of an up-tempo track from her new album. She let the music thrum through her as her four dancers took their places beside her. The words to "Got it Like That" tumbled out of her mouth on autopilot as her body moved to the choreography she'd been practicing nonstop since she came home. The more she danced, the more she got lost in the act of performing and was able to push her emotions behind her. The song ended with Brooke striking a pose onstage, two of her dancers holding her arms as she dipped her body back. They pulled her to her feet and left the stage as Brooke profusely thanked the applauding crowd.

She and her band let the audience have a moment to quiet down before they transitioned into her next song—a slower ballad. Brooke had practiced this song countless times, but she hadn't let herself *experience* it. Until now.

As the opening line filtered out of her mouth, the words hit home in a way they hadn't—or maybe she hadn't let them—

before. When she'd first recorded the song, they'd merely been words. But after all she'd experienced in the last few weeks, they were something much more.

You were a stranger from a faraway dream,
A kind of Prince Charming, who I loved sight unseen.
Just an idea I treasured and craved.
Simply an illusion that didn't even have a name.

You'd slay my dragons,
You'd conquer my heart.
We'd go on adventures,
We'd never be apart.
But you weren't real, boy.
You breathed only in my mind.
Until the day I saw you
And knew you were mine.

The lyrics poured out of her with a passion she'd never felt before. Because for once, the words that had been written for her actually *applied* to her. She figured many little girls dreamed they'd one day meet a man who'd be a game changer for them. Brooke was no exception. She'd spent hours picturing herself in an imaginary relationship that could save her from her family, her career...herself.

Her fingertips had skimmed over the reality of that relationship, but she hadn't been smart enough to grasp it. And now it was gone. All she had left was this song, which she hadn't even written yet but spoke her heart all the same.

Love at first sight isn't real, I know this for sure.
But that doesn't apply to us because we met before.
I knew you from my fantasies, I knew you from my dreams.
I knew before I met you that you were the one for me.

You'd slay my dragons,
You'd conquer my heart.
We'd go on adventures,
We'd never be apart.
But you weren't real, boy.
You breathed only in my mind.
Until the day I saw you
And knew you were mine.

Brooke repeated the chorus again before hitting the final verse with a power she didn't know she had. Without even meaning to, she was making this their song—hers and Cole's. She knew that every time she sang it from that point forward, she'd think about the man who she'd always wished she'd meet but doubted she ever would. About the man who'd walked up to her in a gas station and asked if she'd needed a ride. A man who'd saved her from a predator in a bar but couldn't save her from a future she didn't want.

It didn't register that she'd started crying until she sang the last notes and tasted the saltiness of her tears on her lips. The crowd in front of her blurred through the moisture, and she wasn't sure if they were silent or if she'd been so in the moment that she'd blocked out all sound coming from them. Though she figured it would be pretty hard to hear anything over the screaming of her heart.

She dashed away the tears on her cheeks and did her best to come back to the moment. These clumsy emotions were Brooke Alba's. Brooke Devereaux didn't have time for them.

Before she knew it, the hosts were flanking her and congratulating her on her performance. The crowd was cheering again, and somewhere off to the side, she heard people chanting her name.

"That was amazing, Brooke. So much emotion. Is that song based on anyone in particular?" Danica asked as if they were trading gossip at a slumber party instead of in front of thousands of people.

And even though she wanted to deny it, Brooke was too raw to lie. "It reminds me of someone I used to know."

"Someone special?" Danica prodded with a mischievous grin.

Brooke paused and took in the people surrounding them. She looked off into the wings and saw her parents staring at her with curiosity and maybe a little concern. Not for her well-being, of that Brooke was sure. But she had just bawled on national television, which she'd never done even once before. They probably thought she was losing her mind.

Brooke wasn't sure she'd disagree with that assessment. "Yes," she finally replied.

The single word reply must have held something in it that let the hosts know it wasn't an avenue they should continue to walk down, because Brad quickly changed the subject. "Back to the big news you came here today to share. You ready to share it with the rest of us?"

Letting her gaze skate over the crowd again, Brooke

remembered that she should probably be smiling when she announced that she was joining one of the biggest tours in the country. She felt her cheeks stretch into something she hoped didn't look like a grimace. "I'm assuming you both heard about Jacoby Hale's new tour?" she said with a teasing lightness that belied the riot of nerves that thrummed beneath her skin.

"We certainly have," Danica gushed. "It's set to be the hottest ticket of the year."

"Well, I'm excited to announce that..." Brooke hesitated to swallow the rush of tangy saliva that flooded her mouth. This was the moment that would change everything. There'd been no doubt since she came home what she'd say in this moment, but now that it was time to actually say it, her lips refused to form the words. She cleared her throat and prepared to force the words out.

Her mouth opened to utter the words, when a commotion caught her attention. She looked over and blinked. Then blinked again. And again. Because there was no way what she was seeing was actually there. Or more accurately, *who* she was seeing.

"Brooke!"

She heard her name cut through the crowd as Cole broke through and settled along the metal barrier that separated the crowd from the stage. He rested his hands atop it and looked at her intently. He was there. He'd come.

But what did that mean? She didn't need him to save her now. She'd needed him then—in Wyoming. Needed the support he seemed to be radiating from the crowd. But what good would that do her the next time it came almost a week late? No, Brooke couldn't rely on Cole to save her.

But she sure as shit could rely on herself. "Yeah, I'm sure the tour's going to be awesome. Hopefully it won't sell out before I get to buy a ticket."

The surprise that bloomed over the faces of the hosts was almost comical. Brad stuttered a few times as he clearly struggled to figure out where to go from there. "I, uh, so you... you're not going to *be* on the tour with him?"

This time, Brooke looked over at her parents when she responded. "No. I'm not." The anger was clear in their expressions, but Brooke didn't care. It was freeing in a lot of ways. She'd thoroughly disappointed them on a national stage. There'd be no taking this one back, and that was fine with her.

She turned her head to look back at Cole and couldn't help but laugh. Those fucking dimples got her every time.

CHAPTER SEVENTEEN

When Cole had left the cemetery that day after visiting Jimmy, all he could think about was getting to Brooke. But he was instantly confronted with the issue of *how* to get to her. They'd never exchanged phone numbers, since she'd been using what Cole could only describe as a burner phone for the entirety of their time together, and the last thing they'd thought about when they'd parted ways was keeping in touch.

Then he remembered what she'd said about her appearance on *What's Up, America?*. Cole had looked up the details and made a plan. He hadn't had time to drive across the country to New York, so he'd left Mary Sue in a parking lot at the airport and gotten the first flight out. Upon landing, Cole had tried to figure out a way to reach out to Brooke, but there hadn't been any way to get close to her.

Until her performance in front of the *What's Up, America?* studio. Until he'd pushed his way through the throng of screaming teenagers. Until he'd been stopped dead in his tracks when he'd caught sight of the stage. Because when he'd seen her—and heard her—all the emotions he'd been struggling to keep in check seemed to melt and flood his entire being.

Her song was...beautiful. Just like she was as she sang it. The words sounded like they came from somewhere deep inside, and Cole was entranced by them. Everyone else in the crowd seemed to experience the same reaction, because the noise level dulled to a low murmur as people stared at the stage with rapt attention.

Even when Brooke finished the final line, the crowd remained still as if they wanted to remain in the moment for a bit longer. Cole hardly registered the hosts joining her on stage, but when he heard them mention the Jacoby Hale tour, he forced himself to move.

"Brooke," he yelled as he shoved his way through the crowd.

She didn't appear to have heard him as she responded to one of the hosts.

People in the crowd began to grumble as he forced his way past them, but he didn't care. His focus was singular. "Brooke!"

This time she turned, and her head tilted slightly as her eyes widened. He made his way to the barrier and put his hands on it, contemplating hurtling his body over it so he could stop her from making the mistake he'd basically thrust her into a week ago. But as he watched her—how she stood up straighter, squared her shoulders, and held her head high— Cole felt a calmness move through him that he hadn't felt in... maybe forever. He knew with certainty this was where he was supposed to be, but there was nothing more for him to do.

He'd come. The rest was up to her, just as it always should have been from the beginning of her career.

When Brooke said she wouldn't be going on the tour with that bleach-blond poser Jacoby, Cole's face nearly split in half with the force of his smile as he realized what Brooke was saying. His Princess was finally taking control of her life. Her eyes looked off stage when she confirmed her intention, but she snapped them back to him once she finished. And then she laughed. That crazy girl who'd stolen his heart on the road trip to nowhere was laughing on stage in front of millions of people, and he loved her even more for it.

The hosts were scrambling for things to say, but Brooke interrupted them. "Thank you so much for letting me perform for you today. If you don't mind, I have one more thing I need to do."

The hosts looked relieved that she gave them something to work with. "Of course. What is it?" the female host asked in a voice that was sickeningly sweet.

Brooke pointed into the crowd, right at Cole. "I need to go kiss that man and tell him it's about damn time he got here."

The hosts were taken aback for a second, but they both recovered quickly, obviously realizing what great TV this would make. "Don't let us stop you," the male host said as he swept a hand out toward the crowd.

Brooke didn't waste a second. She hurried down the stairs off to one side and ran through the studio staff that filled the front of the stage.

The entire crowd faded into the background as Cole leaped over the barrier and ran toward Brooke. He half expected one of the many security guards to try to stop him, but not a single person put so much as a hand on him. The distance between them seemed to extend so much that Cole felt it would last forever. But no sooner did he have that thought than Brooke was nearly right in front of him. She leaped, and he caught her, spinning her around as her arms wound around his neck and his tightened around her waist.

Then he slowed, and they each pulled back slightly so they could look at one another. "You came," she said, her voice alight with what sounded like both excitement and disbelief.

"This is where I was always supposed to be," he replied.

"In New York?"

Cole smiled. "With you."

Her answering smile met his in a kiss that deepened as soon as their lips connected.

Cole vaguely heard the collective "Aw" of the crowd, but it didn't stop him. Nothing could have stopped him in that moment. He had the euphoric feeling of floating, like the two of them had transcended gravity and were hovering over the people on the street. Normally such a feeling would have been like a cold bucket of water—that kind of exposure making him vulnerable. But instead, Cole felt empowered by it, and it spurred him on, causing him to tangle his fingers in the hair at the back of her head and devour her mouth.

Their tongues danced, and Cole could almost hear the music between them. The thrum of all they'd been through in such a short time finally finding its rhythm.

Eventually they slowed and awareness of their surroundings came back to them.

"Maybe we should get out of here," Brooke whispered.

"Best idea you've ever had." Cole gave her one more quick kiss before setting her back down on her feet. He looked around in an attempt to figure out how the hell they could get out of there, but a woman wearing a headset appeared out of nowhere and directed them to a tunnel that led inside. He gripped Brooke's hand tightly as they walked, making sure nothing could separate them. They were soon in what Cole assumed was Brooke's dressing room.

Brooke turned toward him and slid her hands around his waist. "I feel like I should be mad at you."

"Well, you've been mad at me for most of the time we've known each other, so there's not much new there."

She tried to fight her smile and lost. "Shut up."

Cole smiled back but then grew serious. "I thought I was doin' the right thing. I really did. You deserve someone who has his shit together. A career, direction, something. But I can't let anyone else have you. You're *mine*. So if I don't deserve you, I'll just have to become someone who does."

"I think I deserve someone who would show up at a live performance in the middle of New York and make out with me on national TV, all so I wouldn't make the biggest mistake of my life. That guy deserves me plenty."

"Oh. Okay then. Pressure's off," Cole teased.

"Such a doofus," she murmured before kissing him.

Cole wasn't sure how long they stayed like that, but it wasn't nearly long enough. They were interrupted by the sound of the door being thrown open and a woman clearing her throat.

"Just what do you think you're doing, Brooke?"

To her credit, Brooke didn't pull away. She pressed one more kiss to Cole's mouth before looking deeply into his eyes. "I'm kissing the boy I love."

Cole didn't know how to describe what zapped through

him, but it was warm and filled him from head to toe.

"What are you talking about?" the woman, who Cole assumed was Brooke's mom, snapped. "How can you love him? You barely even know him."

Brooke's head whipped toward her mother. "Oh yeah. I forgot that you already know who this is. I'm sure Dean told you all about him."

"It's my job to keep you safe, both as your mother and as your agent. You were about to make a huge mistake."

Cole didn't miss the way her mom's eyes glanced over him with disdain as she said the last word.

"Not that you avoided making one anyway. We're going to have to work double-time to undo the mess you made." Brooke's mom crossed her arms over her chest and glared lasers at them.

Brooke wrapped an arm around Cole and leaned into his side. "There's nothing to undo. I'm not going on tour. I'm not recording any more albums. I'm done."

Brooke's mom let out a bitter laugh. "I think you're forgetting that that's not entirely up to you. You have contracts to honor, and—"

"No," Brooke said firmly. "I had a contract to deliver one more album, which has already been recorded. I never signed on for the Jacoby tour, and there's nothing else pending. It's the perfect time to make a clean break."

"What about the contract you have with your father and me?"

Cole was shocked by the words, though he knew he shouldn't have been. Brooke had told him what her mom was like, but it was still jarring to hear the woman disregard Brooke's wishes and throw a contract in her face.

But Brooke's tone was still calm when she replied. "People break contracts with their agents all the time."

Her mom quirked an eyebrow. "Is that really a road you want to go down? Think of how long that could take. The money it would cost."

Shrugging, Brooke replied, "I have plenty of money and nothing but time."

"Oh do you now? Because to my memory, a lot of your money is attached to your *brand*, of which your father and I are an integral part."

"So let me get this straight." Brooke's voice went steely as she took a step toward her mother. Cole moved behind her, hoping she'd be able to feel his support. "You're going to get into a legal battle with your own daughter over money? How do you think that'll look for *your* brand? I'm not sure how many of those new clients you've been signing are going to be too thrilled when they find out you're trying to rip off your own child."

A strange look passed over her mother's face—one that looked a little like fear—but she schooled it quickly. "We'll be able to spin it to our advantage."

Brooke reached back and grabbed Cole's hand, pulling him to stand beside her. "Mom, I want you to meet Cole. My... boyfriend?" she asked as she looked at Cole.

"Hell yeah," he said as he squeezed her hand.

She turned back to her mom. "My boyfriend."

Sighing, her mother said, "I don't particularly care to

meet him after what he's—"

"I've never introduced you to a boyfriend before. Not one you didn't set up for me. This is the first time, in a long time, I'm asking you to share an important moment with me as my mother and not the person in charge of my career. Please. Come meet him."

"I...I..." The hesitance rippled off the woman standing across from them. She seemed completely unaware of what she should do for a few seconds before her professional mask slipped back into place. "I'm being your mother when I tell you how you're throwing everything away for some grifter who'll bleed you dry and leave you all alone somewhere."

Cole had had enough. He was about to open his mouth to give this woman a piece of his mind, when he heard Brooke snort out a laugh. He looked over at her, and the sight of her cracking up caused him to do the same.

Brooke stared at him with so much affection he almost lost himself in the moment. But then she said, "He has no reason to bleed me dry. My skin doesn't even fit him."

Cole let loose a loud laugh as he remembered the words he'd said to her after they'd first met. "You're so warped," he said with as much adoration as he could.

"You said it first," she argued.

That made them both laugh harder, to which her mom asked what the hell was the matter with them.

Cole and Brooke slowly settled down, and Brooke walked over to her mom until she was standing right in front of her. "I know you started this so I could have a career that would make me wealthy and successful. And I can appreciate how hard you worked to make that happen. But"—Brooke let out a deep breath—"I really just want to be happy. You've never once asked me what I want. Never. So I think it's time I told you."

Brooke put her hands on her mom's shoulders. "I want to live, Mom. I want to stay up late watching scary movies and eating pizza and sleep in the next morning without having to worry about recording sessions and learning choreography. I want to hop in the car and drive to nowhere in particular without having to worry about people recognizing me. I want to live a peaceful, boring life where I teach little kids how to dance and enjoy arguing with the man of my dreams. I know it's not the life *you* want for me. But can you at least respect that it's the one *I* want?"

Cole saw Brooke's mom's eyes fill with water, but no tears ever fell. "You'll regret it." It wasn't a threat but a simple warning from a woman who thought she knew better.

"I won't."

Her mom took a shuddering breath and gently shook herself free of Brooke's hands. "I guess we'll have to agree to disagree. We'll let you out of your contract as long as you don't discuss any...unfavorable opinions with anyone."

Cole saw Brooke's shoulders sag, and he moved up and wrapped an arm protectively around her. How dare this woman continue to treat Brooke like a business deal after everything that had just been said?

Brooke merely nodded. Her mom turned and went to the door, pulling it open. "Goodbye, Mom," Brooke said softly.

"Goodbye, Brooke." Her mom's voice was wooden as she yanked the door closed behind her.

Turning instantly in his arms, Brooke buried her face in his chest and cried. Cole held her and let her get it all out, rubbing circles on her back and whispering how wonderful she was and how thankful he was that she chose him.

Eventually the tears stopped and Brooke pulled away, wiping her eyes. "Those will be the last tears I'll ever cry for that woman."

Cole knew they probably wouldn't be, but he kept his mouth shut.

"I should change. And then I should probably call my accountant and make sure my parents don't do anything with my money. Then I guess... Jesus, I don't even know what else I need to do. Get my stuff from my parents' house maybe?"

Cole could tell she was starting to get overwhelmed, so he silenced her with a kiss. "How about we start with you getting changed? Then we'll get a cab and go back to my hotel room. I agree that you should probably call your accountant as soon as you can, but everything else can probably wait."

"Wait for what?"

"For me to show you how much I missed you."

"Mm, does that show involve a bed?"

"Bed, couch, wall. Whatever."

Brooke giggled. "We better get going then." But instead of moving away, she pressed in closer to him, which had his dick instantly perking up.

"Don't tease me, Princess. I'll create a scandal right here in this dressing room."

"Promises, promises," she said as she trailed soft kisses along the scruff on his jaw.

"Brooke," he bit out.

"Yes?" she replied.

"Wherever we get naked is where I intend to stay for at least the next two days. So unless you want to be stuck here, then I suggest you get a move on."

With a sigh, she took a step back. "Fine. Have it your way."

"Oh, baby. I intend to."

CHAPTER EIGHTEEN

Brooke barely stepped inside the room before Cole had her up against the door and was kissing the ever-loving fuck out of her. Lifting one of her legs, she attempted to climb him until he got with the program and lifted her. She could feel the hard press of his cock through his jeans, and she wanted it inside her immediately.

The drive to the hotel had been an exercise in restraint. She'd had the studio call a private car for them so she could make her phone calls from the back seat, since she knew she wouldn't be able to focus on business once she had Cole alone in a bedroom. After getting her finances as squared away as they could be without face-to-face meetings and filling out a shit ton of paperwork, Brooke was ready to reacquaint herself with every square inch of Cole's body.

His hands squeezed her ass through her leggings as she writhed against him. Trailing kisses down her neck, Cole let out a long groan. "Missed you," he murmured against her skin.

"You too. Need you naked."

At her words, Cole tightened his hold on her and spun them before walking toward the bed. He lowered her onto it and then reached down and whipped off her shoes, followed by her burgundy tights.

She helped him out by pulling off her cream tunic. Arching her back, she reached around to unclasp her sheer white bra, but Cole stopped her.

"Leave everything else on." His voice was deep and needy, and it turned her on like nothing else ever had. He quickly stripped out of his jeans and burnt-orange T-shirt. His cock poked out of his briefs, causing her to shudder with anticipation. Finally, pushing down that last piece of fabric so it fell to the floor, he stood gloriously naked in front of her.

He really was otherworldly. The hard ridge of his abs, the compact bunching of his muscles, the squareness of his jaw, and the rugged symmetry of his face made for a man who could've graced the covers of men's magazines if he'd been so inclined. But instead, he chose to be holed up in a hotel room with her. Brooke would've asked what was wrong with him, except she didn't want to risk him coming to his senses. Because the man was *hers*. And she wasn't ever being separated from him again.

Cole lowered himself on top of her, balancing his weight on his forearms. He kissed her deeply, his tongue tangling with hers.

"Cole. Please," she begged. Her clit throbbed every time he rocked his cock against her pussy. There was no doubt he'd slide into her smoothly and gloriously, considering how wet she was.

He didn't respond with words, but his hand moved down to slide her thong to the side. And as he guided himself to her entrance and slid inside, Brooke couldn't hold back the moan of pleasure.

"Feels so fucking good," he muttered as he thrust into her.

"Not gonna be able to go slow."

"No slow. Slow bad," she replied, not even caring that she sounded like a moron.

He picked up the pace, his cock moving in and out of her at a speed that made her inch up the bed with every push. Lowering his head, he licked her nipples through her bra as he rode her.

The combination of sensations had her orgasm building rapidly. But when he lowered one of his hands so he could massage her clit, she was a goner. Her body heaved and bucked as if she'd been hit by a freight train.

Cole continued to pump into her, his breathing harsh against her skin. She wrapped her arms tightly around him, wanting to be as close to him as possible when he released inside of her.

"Oh fuck, oh fuck, oh fuck," he chanted as he thrust into her a few more times before pushing himself deep inside. She felt his cock pulse as he came. He'd pushed up onto his hands, and she could see how the muscles in his neck and arms flexed as his orgasm hit him. He gave a few more shallow thrusts before his body relaxed a bit.

Lowering his head, he captured her lips in another kiss before he pulled out and plopped down next to her. She instantly turned toward him and laid her head on his chest. His arm wrapped around her, and they rested like that for a bit, giving themselves time to come back to earth.

After a while, Brooke had half dozed off when Cole spoke. "So what's next?"

Brooke sighed, none too happy to have her post-sex

happy bubble burst. "I'll need to stay in the city for a couple more days to get things squared away with the accountant and my lawyer. After that, we can do whatever we want."

"I'm gonna need to go back to Oregon. I left Mary Sue there. She's probably pissed that I ditched her for another woman."

Brooke laughed softly against his skin.

Cole cleared his throat. "I wasn't sure if...you know...if you wanted to go back there with me. Or if you wanted me to come back here. Or...what."

Babbling Cole was almost as sexy as naked Cole. "Well, you do still owe me a trip to Arches Park. I figure Oregon is much closer to it than New York is."

Cole released a breath.

Brooke realized he must have been nervous to hear her response. "What? Did you think I was going to let you out of my sight?" Brooke let out a mocking laugh. "Silly boy. You're stuck with me now."

"That's everything I could want."

His words did funny things to her heart. There were pieces of her that sometimes seemed as if they were fundamentally broken. But then Cole said sweet shit like that, and Brooke felt almost normal. Like she hadn't just said what may have been a permanent goodbye to her mother an hour before. Like she hadn't just walked away from a multi-million-dollar opportunity to instead travel the country in a pickup truck. Like she hadn't put all of her trust in some guy she met at a gas station in the middle of nowhere.

Or maybe doing all of those things *was* normal. Maybe

taking the road that had been mapped out for her would have been the crazy decision. It didn't matter either way. Because regardless of what anyone thought, Brooke knew that while she may not have made the most responsible decision, she had made the right one.

"I love you," Cole whispered into her ear as he hugged her close.

Brooke vowed to take every chance, risk every decision, and challenge every fear in order to go on every adventure she could with the wonderful former stranger next to her. And she did this with the words she swore she'd say every day for the rest of her life. "I love you too."

BONUS EPILOGUE
FOR MISADVENTURES WITH MY ROOMMATE

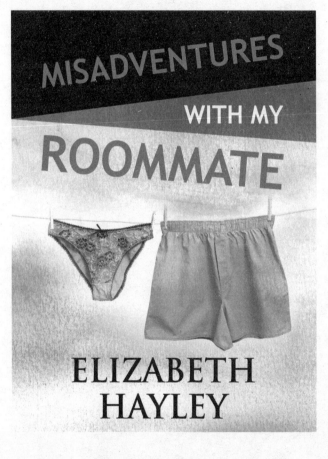

Keep reading for special bonus content!

BONUS EPILOGUE FOR
MISADVENTURES WITH MY ROOMMATE

Blake wasn't sure what was going on with Gavin, but he'd better figure his shit out soon or she was going to dump him for a vibrator. He'd been distant for the past week, and she had *needs*, dammit. Granted, he had a show coming up that promised to be a big deal. A local art critic would be there, and Gavin had been obsessing over the presentation of the photos in his collection ever since he'd heard that news.

But that didn't explain why he didn't want to get his freak on. Wasn't sex supposed to relax people who were stressed out? He should be all over her like he had been every other day of the eight months they'd officially been together.

"Why aren't you all over me?" she asked as she jerked the shower curtain back, revealing a wet and naked Gavin.

"Uh, what?" Gavin said as his hands paused in the act of rubbing shampoo into his hair.

Blake's eyes moved down his defined chest, the ridges in his abs, and the hardening cock that would soon be jutting out from his body like a rhino horn.

"Blake?" Gavin said, a tone of humor in his voice.

"Huh?" she mumbled, her eyes never leaving that cock she wanted buried deep in her body.

"Eyes up here, babe."

"No thanks. My eyes are fine right where they are."

"It's difficult to talk to you while you're eying my dick like it's a lollipop."

She did look at him then. "I'm not asking you to talk. Except for that filthy stuff you whisper to me while you're fucking me. You can talk like that all you want."

"I have to be at work in half an hour."

"Pfft, it's not going to take me nearly that long to get off. It's been *days*." Blake had already started stripping, and she was overjoyed to see Gavin track her movements with his eyes. When he gave his cock a long, slow stroke, Blake knew she had him.

Once all her clothes were pooled around her feet, she joined him in the shower. His arms went around her automatically and *that*, she realized, was what she'd been missing more than anything else. Blake hadn't let herself depend on very many people in her life—didn't give many people a chance to get close. But Gavin was different. He always had been. And now that she knew he'd prop her up when she needed to lean on him, she'd grown addicted to the feeling.

She tilted her head toward him and he kissed her immediately, his tongue sweeping into her mouth like it longed to be there. The kiss was deep and consuming, and Blake wouldn't have ever wanted it to stop except that she wanted to be fucked by him even more than she wanted to be kissed by him.

Slowly turning around, she backed up into him so his

cock was nestled between her ass cheeks, and she began to grind against him erotically.

His hands slipped around her and cupped her breasts, squeezing them before letting his fingers tweak her nipples.

A groan left her lips as she dropped her head back against his chest, giving him the opportunity to suck at the soft skin on her collarbone. Letting a hand dip below her stomach and between her legs, she fondled her throbbing clit. She hadn't been joking before. This wasn't going to take her long. But she didn't want her own finger to make her come apart. She wanted Gavin's cock to do that.

She bent over at the waist and put her hands firmly against the shower wall. Spreading her legs, she offered herself up to Gavin, who wasted no time. He let his finger slip inside her for a moment before lining up his rock-hard shaft and pushing in.

The moan that left her made her sound slutty, and it was the most empowering feeling ever. Because she could be slutty and needy and wanton with this man because he got off on it. And being wanted by Gavin made her feel powerful. For someone who'd always felt comfortable in her own skin, the feeling of imperviousness that welled within her when she was with Gavin hadn't made sense at first. But she quickly came to understand that being loved for who you were was like coating your bones with titanium. What had been strong before was now invincible.

The rhythmic snapping of Gavin's hips set up a quick, satisfying rhythm, and Blake unraveled quickly.

"So fucking sexy," Gavin growled behind her as his

hands gripped her hips more firmly.

Blake used her hands to push herself back to meet each thrust. The slapping of their skin was obscene and the most perfect soundtrack Blake could imagine for this moment.

"Fuck, I'm gonna come. You there with me, baby?" he asked.

Hell yes, she was. But the only sound she was capable of making were the moans of pleasure that rumbled out of her throat.

Gavin thrust hard twice more, and that was all it took for her body to convulse with her orgasm. His pace stuttered behind her, and he began chanting, "Oh, fuck," until he pushed deeply one final time and emptied his release inside her.

They stayed that way for a few moments, Gavin seated deep within her and Blake still bent over. Her legs were a bit shaky, but her back felt locked in place as if her orgasm had frozen her.

Gavin slipped out and pulled her to a stand, which caused a bit of a twinge in her lower back, but she was thankful for the assistance. Without him, she likely would have stayed stuck like that all day.

"I love you," Gavin whispered in her ear before nipping her lobe.

"Love you too." She sighed a deep, content kind of sigh before leaning back against his chest.

"I'm sorry I've been distracted."

"S'okay," she replied. And it was. Mostly. "We should make a mold of your dick so I can bang it the next time you get distracted."

And as Gavin laughed, she wondered how to tell him she wasn't even remotely kidding.

◆ ◆ ◆ ◆

Gavin was nervous. Thankfully The Coffee Bean was slow today, so he'd had a chance to practice the design he'd been working on perfecting for the past few weeks. Stu would've freaked if he'd known how much coffee Gavin had wasted, but what Stu didn't know wouldn't hurt him.

Blake's shift was due to start in ten minutes, and Gavin's heart was beating so furiously, he thought someone might actually be able to see it pounding through his chest.

He got rid of his last attempt, content that it looked as good as it possibly could. Then he busied himself tidying up the counter. There was a lull in customers, which was good. Other than a few people sprinkled about, everything was calm. Calm until a tiny hurricane came in through the door.

"You're not even going to believe what just happened," Blake said, her eyes wide and a little wild.

"What?" Gavin asked. "Here, let me make you a drink."

"Unless you have alcohol back there, a drink isn't going to cut it. You're never going to guess who I saw."

"Probably not, so you should just skip to the part where you tell me," he said as he walked toward the latte machine.

"I just ran into your *mom*. And in case you were wondering, she definitely still hates me."

Gavin quickly turned around at that. "Why? What did she say?" If his mom had been rude to Blake, he would lose his shit. Ever since he'd told his parents he was going to live his life the way he saw fit, they'd barely spoken to him. But his mom had called a couple of times to check in and ask if he was still with "that girl."

That was typically around the time Gavin hung up on her. He wondered what she was even doing in the city. Sure, she met people for lunch now and again, but the odds of running into Blake would have been infinitesimal.

"Nothing. But I'm pretty sure she put a curse on me with her eyes. If I get hit by a bus, you better tell the cops to search her house for a voodoo doll of me with pins in it."

Gavin almost pointed out that it likely wouldn't have pins in it if she was killed by a bus, but that would open up a whole other line of discussion he didn't want to venture down. "So she didn't say anything?"

"She said hello and called me Brenda. A real passive aggressive aficionado that woman is." Blake smiled, which let Gavin relax. Blake had the thickest skin of anyone he'd ever met, and she seemed to get a special thrill from the fact his parents didn't like her. He didn't understand but was thankful for it all the same.

"I don't want to talk about her anymore," he said as he cast a look over his shoulder at Blake. "She doesn't deserve to even breathe the same air as you."

"Sweet talker," she said as she propped her elbow on the counter and rested her chin on her hand.

He turned back to the machine and finished his task. Once it was done, he took a deep breath and steeled himself. This was it. The moment he'd been planning for weeks—the one he'd obsessed over before finally deciding this was the most *them* way to do this. He just hoped it went how he'd pictured it. He carried the drink over to her, his shaking hands making him afraid he was going to drop the damn thing. "I've been working on a new design. I wanted to ask you what you thought." He set the cup down in front of her and held his breath.

Blake looked down at the drink in front of her, and then her eyes widened and darted to his. "Gavin, holy shit."

He would've sworn he could feel every pulse point in his body. She looked shocked, but was it a good shocked or a bad shocked? "What do you think?"

"I think Stu is going to fire you if you start drawing cock rings on his lattes."

Gavin's brain shorted out. "Wait...what?"

"I'm not saying it's not impressive or anything. But, and I'm not sure I've ever said this to someone else, it's not really appropriate."

Gavin rubbed his face with his hands. "It's not a cock ring," he said, whispering the final two words.

"Oh." She looked at the latte again and then back at him. "I'm confused."

Gavin gestured for her to move away from the counter before he put his hands on it and catapulted himself over to her side.

"That was super hot. You should do that when we go home later," Blake remarked.

"You're not allowed to talk anymore for a second," he said, his tone teasing.

"That's even hotter," she whispered.

Gavin laughed. "You're ridiculous." He grabbed the drink he'd made her in one hand and took her hand with his other. "This is a grande quad nonfat one-pump no-whip mocha latte."

Blake's face screwed up at the mention of her drink nemesis.

"And the design is not a cock ring. It's an engagement ring."

It took Blake a minute to register his words, but he could tell when she did. Her eyes widened again and filled with tears. "The cock ring made more sense," she said, her voice almost a whimper.

He noticed the café had gone quiet, and he felt eyes on them, but he let all of that fall away. He leaned in close to her. "No, it doesn't," he said against her lips before kissing her. Then he put the cup down and dropped to one knee. He reached into his apron pocket and withdrew a small box. He struggled to open the lid with one hand but finally managed. He held it out so she could see it.

She gripped his other hand tightly as she gazed at the ring in his hand. "You want to marry me?" she said, and she sounded so vulnerable in that moment that Gavin swore he'd spend the rest of his life protecting and cherishing her.

"Shouldn't I be the one asking that question?" he said with a smirk before he grew more serious. "Of course. There is no one else in this world like you. Which means there's no one else in this world for me. You're my best friend and my soulmate. Not to mention we're already roommates," he teased. "It just makes good sense for us to get married."

She smiled at that, a single tear making a track down her cheek.

"What do you say?" he asked.

"I say *yes*. For you, the answer will always be yes."

And as Gavin slipped the ring on her finger and then stood and swept her up into his arms, he knew the answer would always be yes for her too.

ACKNOWLEDGMENTS

We of course have to thank Meredith Wild for liking our writing enough to bring us on to the Misadventures team. You've been a friend to us since the beginning, and we're eternally grateful for that.

To Scott, Robyn, and the editing team, thank you for all of your hard work and kind words. You're so great at what you do, and you're a pleasure to work with.

To the rest of the Waterhouse Press team, thank you for your continued support and for designing all of the kickass covers and graphics.

Sarah Younger, thank you for...everything. For letting us vent, for being unapologetically honest, and for always looking out for us.

The Padded Room, thank you for supporting our craziness. From posting links, teasers, and helping get our name out there, you are a vital part of our dreams. We love you ladies!

To our families, we're not sure how all of you put up with us so we can keep riding along on this journey, but we love you for that and a million other reasons. Thank you :)

MORE MISADVENTURES